A Rich Aftertaste

The Coffee Shop Romance Series, Volume 1

Lexy Timms

Published by Dark Shadow Publishing, 2022.

This is a work of fiction. Similarities to real people, places, or events are entirely coincidental.

A RICH AFTERTASTE

First edition. September 2, 2022.

Copyright © 2022 Lexy Timms.

Written by Lexy Timms.

A RICH AFTERTASTE

USA TODAY BESTSELLING AUTHOR

LEXY TIMMS

Copyright 2022
By Lexy Timms

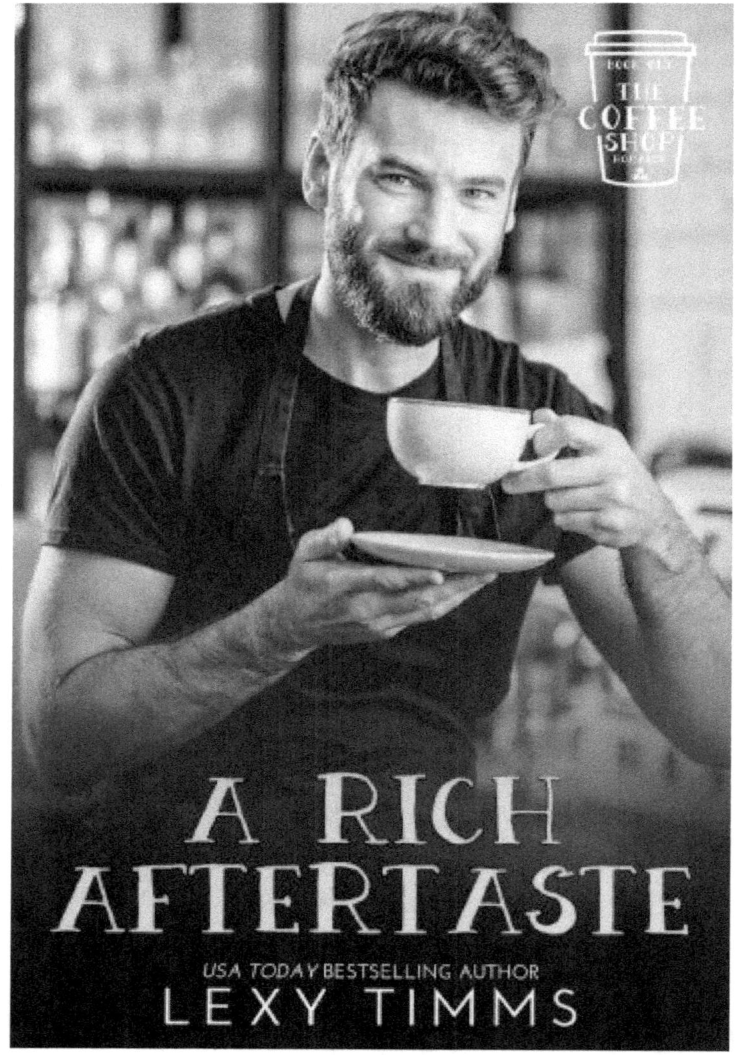
A RICH
AFTERTASTE
USA TODAY BESTSELLING AUTHOR
LEXY TIMMS

All rights reserved.
A Rich Aftertaste
The Coffee Shop Romance Series #1
Copyright 2022
By Lexy Timms
Cover by: Book Cover by Design[1]

The Coffee Shop Romance

A Rich After Taste
A Bitter Flavor
Baked to Perfection

Find Lexy Timms:

Lexy Timms Newsletter:
http://www.lexytimms.com/newsletter
Lexy Timms Facebook Page:
https://www.facebook.com/LexyTimmsAuthor
Lexy Timms Website:
http://www.lexytimms.com

Want to read more...
For **FREE?**
Sign up for Lexy Timms' newsletter
And she'll send you updates on new releases, ARC copies of books
and a whole lotta fun!
Sign up for news and updates!
http://www.lexytimms.com/newsletter

A Rich Aftertaste Blurb

Coffee spelled backwards is eeffoc – and I don't give effoc until I've had my coffee...

Nick Sullivan knows the value of hard work, and after a windfall from a family member comes his way, he finally realizes his dream of opening a coffee shop and bakery.

Becoming the hot spot for the newly built apartment building in the heart of the city, he finds himself extremely successful and with offers left and right to expand and franchise that he routinely ignores. But when he meets a girl who moves into one of the apartments above his shop, Nick starts to realize something might be missing from his life. When she enlists him to help with her friend's wedding, the two-start developing a relationship that could rock his carefully constructed life in more ways than one!

Alexis—known as Alex to her friends—comes from a wealthy family, but isn't interested in the kind of life they lead.

Rather than being a trophy wife, she wants to have a career, and despite their constant pressure, she strikes out on her own to get it. When she moves into the new apartment building and runs into Nick, she finds herself both hopelessly attracted to him and also needing his help for her best friend's wedding disaster in progress. But when she starts to mix her business mind with her love life, things get muddy quick. Can she keep the two aspects of her life baking away, or will she burn one, or both, to a crisp?

Chapter One

Alexis

Phones ring exactly when I don't want them to.

Like during meetings. Or when I'm trying to talk with the executives who have come down from their towering offices to the jungle of cubicles and the smaller offices to check in with the rest of us. Right as I'm finally figuring out a problem I've been having with a project and trying to get it untangled so I have some hope of finishing it.

That was the way it was that afternoon. I'd been standing, considering myself on my way out the door, for the last forty minutes, and no matter how hard I tried to take that next step, I wasn't making any progress. First, it was the owner of a company I'd been trying to land as a client and had been playing coy and not making any decisions but chose that day to suddenly have a million questions he absolutely had to ask in individual phone calls. Then it was an existing client who needed me to talk them through a simple shift in their budget we'd already discussed twice that week. After that, a prospective client who was finally getting back to me after I'd been waiting for their call for days.

It was one of those days. Of course, it was. Of all days, that had to be the one that was going to be a pain in my ass. The one time I was trying to leave the office early to do something that wasn't work, I was suddenly wading through all the projects and calls and conversations that should have happened when I was spinning around in my office chair waiting for any of it to happen. That was a common feeling for me. Even when I had plenty to do, I was looking for something else. I was never willing to settle or to feel like I had done enough. I always worked as hard as I could, trying to do more every day.

People on the outside often used words like *driven* and *determined* to describe me, but I felt like it was more than that. I wasn't just trying to accomplish something. I was trying to prove it. I was constantly chasing after that sense of legitimacy. I had to prove I could make it, to be a success in my own right rather than relying on the established reputation and wealth of my family. That was the thing. I had a whole life waiting for me from the time I was born. It was written in the stars. Or the ancestry papers, as it were.

All I had to do was be the good little girl that was expected of me. Behave, be polite, and eventually marry the wealthy man my family thought was right for me and be the dutiful wife. It wasn't as oppressive as it sounded. For some people, that is. I knew a lot of women my age who were very happy to spend their lives pursuing interests and enjoyment rather than careers, essentially being a professional wife, mother, and hostess. And more power to them. If that was what they wanted, I believed whole-heartedly that was what they should have. It wasn't that there was something intrinsically wrong with the whole concept.

It just wasn't right for me.

From the time I was really young, I knew I wanted a career. I wanted something that made me stand out from my family. Growing up only being looked at as the next generation of my family was too small. I was barely in double digits when I realized that also meant that everything I ever accomplished would come under question. When you grow up the child of wealth, power, and influence, people tend to forget you have your own capabilities and pursuits. They believe anything you ever do or want is simply handed to you. And I didn't want that. I wanted to be successful and recognized because I did something for myself.

So I focused hard in school. I went on to get an advanced degree and threw myself fully into my career, always trying to build it and get it to the next level.

But that meant I was always busy and stressed, especially now that I was also helping one of my best friends prepare for her wedding and another prepare for the impending birth of her first child. While also looking to move into a new home because I had officially had enough of the nosy neighbors and frustrating commute that came along with the old apartment building where I was currently living.

That was exactly why I needed to get out of work early that day. I had finally managed to land a viewing appointment for an apartment at a gorgeous building I had been coveting since it first went up more than a year before. The apartments had filled up in an instant then, and I put myself on a waiting list more as motivation and a vision board item than because I actually thought I was going to have a chance of getting in any time soon. After all, this wasn't the kind of building someone would just move out of on a whim when they got an apartment. People who managed to move in here stayed.

But thank goodness for old age.

Saying that probably wasn't my best look.

Right then, though, I didn't care that the apartment had recently been home to a woman now wandering the other side. As long as she wasn't still in the living room where she died, I was happy. I just needed to make sure I got to my appointment on time. The waiting list went on long after my name, so if I wasn't there, they could easily just pick up the phone, call the next name, and I could be attending a housewarming rather than a viewing by the time I got across town.

I finally managed to run out of the building and toward my car, but my phone was ringing by the time I opened the door. I glanced at the screen and let out a sigh before answering.

"Hello, Mother," I said.

"You know, Alexis, you really should work on sounding more pleasant when you answer the phone. You never know who could be on the other end," my mother said.

I hated that she called me Alexis.

"I do know who is on the other end, Mother," I said, climbing into the car. "That's the beauty of caller ID."

"So you chose to be that unpleasant when you saw it was me?" she asked.

Damn. Busted. It doesn't matter how old we get; mothers are still mothers.

"I'm sorry. I didn't mean to be unpleasant. It's just a really stressful day for me," I said, pulling out into traffic.

"Then you must be thinking about Gabriela's wedding." I wasn't, but that wasn't going to register to her even if I said it, so I wasn't going to bother. "I have been, too. It's getting so close. I'm sure she's just overwhelmed with all the last-minute details. Her mother says she hasn't even finished her thank you notes from her bridal shower yet. You know, as her maid of honor, it really is your responsibility to make sure she stays calm and help her through all of these things."

"I know what my responsibility is. We already have a plan for the thank you notes," I said.

"How about the wedding? Do you have a date yet? The maid of honor can't come to the wedding without a date."

"What kind of rule is that? Maryellen went to her cousin Stacy's wedding without a date," I said.

"And people talked about her the whole time," Mom pointed out.

"People would have talked about her no matter what. That's kind of the problem with groups of these kinds of people. They talk about each other," I said. "And don't you think they already talk about me?"

"Yes, honey," she said in that faux gentle tone mothers must get bestowed upon them before being allowed out of the maternity ward, "I know they do. Do we really need to give them something else to wonder about?"

"The wedding is about Gabriela and Dean," I said. "Why does it matter if I show up with anyone and who that might be?"

"It's just how things are done, Alexis," she said. "You don't want attention being pulled to you because you look like a single woman."

"I am a single woman," I said.

"And perhaps there's a reason for that," she said. "It's difficult to find the right man when your nose is in your work all the time."

"I happen to like my work."

"As you've told me. But maybe you could at least put a little more thought into your appearance. When I saw you the other day, you looked like you'd barely put any thought into your outfit, and you weren't even wearing lipstick. It concerns me that you aren't taking proper care of yourself."

"Mom, I was in the middle of a jog. I don't wear full makeup when I'm working out," I said.

"But you could. There are plenty of good brands that offer waterproof options. I'm sure they would work for sweat. If you insist on going out in public to work out, you should at least put some effort into how you're presenting yourself. You could meet the most wonderful man while jogging, you know."

"If I'm meeting a man while jogging, it's probably because he's jogging, too, and he's not going to expect me to be in makeup," I said.

"It certainly would be a lovely surprise for him if you were," she said.

And thus went my conversation with my mother that took up the entirety of my way across town. She wasn't mean. She was rarely actually mean. She had just perfected the art of being nagging and annoying and focusing in on the exact elements of myself and my life that, though I loathe using such an overdone word, triggered me.

She had so perfected the art, in fact, that she had transitioned away from her displeasure at my uncoordinated jogging outfit and sweaty hair to what she deemed my "unstable living situation" right as I was pulling into the reserved parking spot near what I hoped would be my new apartment building.

"Mom, I'm not going to become a transient. In fact, I've got to go. I have an apartment to look at in the Bentley," I said.

"The Bentley," Mom said, sounding dangerously close to being impressed. "Oh, yes, Marla Vandross died."

"Yep. Lucky me. I've got to go. I'll talk to you soon," I said.

She was saying something as I ended the call, but I had approximately thirty-seven seconds to get into the lobby and look put together, and I wasn't wasting any of it.

No matter how many times I saw it, the Bentley took my breath away. It was gorgeous and just felt like something. Like if you lived there, you were somebody. I felt hopeful as I walked into the lobby. This was my next step.

Almost immediately, a polished-looking man with a smile that rivaled the gleaming marble of the floor came striding toward me. His hand was out before he was within ten feet, and I had a moment of not knowing if I was supposed to walk toward him or stay where I was.

"Ms. Murphy," he said. "I'm Grayson Barrett."

"Alex," I said, shaking his hand.

"Alex. Welcome to the Bentley. I'll be showing you around," I said.

I smiled and nodded. "Thank you. I'm really excited to be here."

"Well, there is a lot to be excited about living here. I like to think of it as living in a top-quality resort. We offer a wide variety of amenities to our residents, starting with The Coffee Shop right here in the lobby."

He gestured to the side, and I saw a little shop in the lobby. I thought he was just referring to it being a coffee shop, but the sign hanging over the door declared that the actual name. It made me smile again. It was charming. As Grayson described the growing popularity of the shop and the regulars that frequented it, I peered through the floor-to-ceiling glass walls surrounding it.

The energetic tour guide had moved on to talk about something else, but I missed it. I was too busy watching the extremely attractive barista behind the counter.

"Alex?"

Grayson's voice snapped me back into reality, and I realized he'd already started walking across the lobby toward the elevator. Within the hour, I had toured the apartment, fallen completely in love just the way I expected to, and signed the lease. I walked out of the building ready for my new chapter.

Chapter Two

Nick

That Wednesday was pretty much just like every other day. And that was just the way I liked it.

Just about every day found me right where I was standing then, behind the counter at The Coffee Shop. Opening that little shop was my dream, and I had put everything into it. All my time, energy, and money had gone into starting it up and making something of it. I even lost my long-term relationship because I was so devoted to starting the shop.

It was all one hundred percent worth it, though, and once it was open, it only got better. I was happy to get there early to bake the pastries and other food on the menu, spend the day serving coffee, then stay late into the evening to make more food or plan new things. It was everything to me.

Not that I did it all completely on my own. I did have two employees who came in for a few hours during the week so I wasn't working nonstop. It didn't always stop me. It wasn't unusual for me to just stay there while they were working, even when I didn't actually need to.

It wasn't just the work itself or my devotion to the business I'd worked so hard to build that kept me at the shop for long hours. In the little less than two years since I'd opened, I'd picked up quite a few regulars who made a point to visit my shop every day. Sometimes twice.

They'd talk to me about their lives, and I was there for them however I could be, even if that was just making them a special treat or keeping their coffee topped off while they vented about whatever was bothering them.

It felt like being the caffeine and baked goods version of a neighborhood bartender, and I never wanted to leave any of them in a lurch. If they were going to put forth the effort to make my shop a part of their day and their life, the least I could do was be there.

One of those regulars was sitting in his usual spot at the counter. Barry was a particularly colorful person, in appearance and in personality. He had an affinity toward bold patterns and fabrics that didn't go together in any real way, but apparently their completely haphazard association was what put them on the absolute cutting edge of fashion. When it came to his personality, Barry was all hand gestures, fast talking, and constant energy. He was the type I could see making some people very nervous, but I saw the positive in him. I didn't know how much I'd be able to take in long stretches, but the small doses I got each day were a bright spot.

That day, he was all about his new puppy. Apparently, the acquisition of said puppy wasn't something Barry had planned. As he put it, the universe had led them together, and their paths intersected at the exact right point to ensure they would go forward on this journey of life side by side. As it turned out, that exact right point was actually a literal intersection near a park, and there was a slight possibility the universe leading them together was actually an unintended puppy-napping from a nearby breeder after a breakout.

But since it had been a full twenty-four hours and the breeder hadn't straight-out said they were missing a puppy, Barry was taking it as a sign they were destined for each other. Possible inadvertent felony aside, I was happy for him and the obvious adoration he had for his new little family member. I decided that night I would make some special treats to give him the next day to welcome the puppy home.

Barry had just gotten into his case for me allowing Banana Split into the shop in the tradition of pub dogs when Grayson walked through the door. The only real way to describe the way he carried himself was swagger. A representative of the company that owned the Bentley, Grayson was responsible for renting out the apartments and then seeing to the needs of the tenants once they were in place. He put a tremendous amount of significance into that role, which in turn gave him a massively self-important air. The fact that he went through women faster than my customers went through coffee and had no qualms about giving all the details and moving on without any emotion didn't help.

He wasn't all bad. Maybe it was just that I tried to see the good in people, but he could be funny, and he seemed to genuinely take pride in doing well at his job. But when he walked into The Coffee Shop that afternoon, I knew I wasn't in for a heartwarming story about him finding the perfect theater tickets to help a couple celebrate their anniversary or how he was helping organize the tenants for a charity fundraising event. This was going to be about his most recent conquest.

"Hey, Grayson," I said when he dropped down onto one of the stools at the counter. "Want your usual?"

"Absolutely," he said. I made him his extra sweet hazelnut caramel coffee with two espresso shots and set it in front of him. "Thanks. Did you see that girl I just showed the apartment to?"

He didn't even wait until after his first sip of coffee. That was almost impressive if it wasn't also a bit sleazy.

"No, I didn't," I said.

I tried not to put any kind of emotion into the words so he couldn't interpret it as encouragement, but he didn't need any. Grayson would probably talk about women to the empty shop if we weren't here to listen to him. It was compulsive. Like breathing.

"She was so hot. Like..."—he searched for the right assortment of adjectives to describe her—"ridiculously hot."

Apparently he was short on vocabulary that day.

"Must have missed her," I said.

"Too bad. She was amazing. She had this whole corporate sexy thing happening. Like any second she was just going to tear off her blouse, hop up on a desk, and lecture me about the budget crisis."

Somewhere in his confusion about whether this woman was an executive, a professor, or a government entity, a few new customers came in, and I stepped out of the conversation to take their orders. The time it took to make their drinks and get their food wasn't enough to cool Grayson off, and the second I got back in his orbit, he was talking about her again. "Her" because he never bothered to mention her name. I figured it was entirely possible he had already forgotten her name. Grayson wasn't big on actually getting to know any of the women he pursued. As soon as he bedded them once or twice, he was done and moved on.

Usually, I didn't consider it any of my business. After all, he was a grown man, and he went after grown women. How they handled things between them was just that. Between them. It wasn't really up to me to judge him or try to make decisions for anyone else. But this was the first time he had intentions of going after a woman who lived in the building. That changed things.

"You know, Grayson, maybe it's not such a great idea for you to pursue anything with this woman. Someone who works for the company that owns the building dating someone who is applying to live in that building could really look sketchy," I said. "It might seem like you are trying to coerce her or using the fact that she wants the apartment as a bargaining chip."

Grayson took a swig of his coffee and flashed me a grin. "No worries about that. She already signed the lease and is moving in this weekend. And I didn't even say anything to her during the whole thing, so there's no risk of her thinking anything like that. It's smooth sailing."

"I don't know if I'd go that far," I said. "In fact, her living here just keeps up the complication. You really should be careful, Grayson. You could be charged with sexual harassment."

Grayson stared at me over the edge of his cup for a second, then burst into laughter like he thought the warning was the funniest commentary he'd ever heard.

"Well, it's not harassment if she's receptive to it, so I guess we'll just have to wait and see, won't we?" he asked. He took the last sip of his coffee, tossed some money on the counter, and gave me a wave. "All right. I'm out of here. Thanks for the coffee. See you tomorrow."

I watched him leave, shaking my head and pondering what type of HR hell he was going to bring raining down on the building. Maybe things would work out. The new tenant might be smart enough to reject his advances and things would just blow over.

Barry stayed at the shop a little longer, doing what he usually did and lingering well after everyone else had already left. Sometimes he managed to find his way out the door before the 5:30 closing time listed on the sign. Sometimes he didn't. It didn't really matter. I decided when I was actually going to close, and the vast majority of the time, I didn't hit that time. That day, he was out only twenty minutes past closing time, and I locked the door behind him so no one else wandered in expecting coffee and food.

But it wasn't time to leave yet. Locking up just meant I could go into the kitchen and focus on making a few things. First up on the list was the peanut butter oatmeal treats I had in mind for Banana Split. They were shaped like dog bones, but they were essentially just cookies so Barry could have a snack with the puppy if he wanted to. While those were baking, I took a basket and filled it with all the leftover pastries, sandwiches, and other food from the shop from the day. Then I went to work making a few dozen cookies and a batch of sourdough crackers.

When it was all finished, I took the basket and headed out. It would only be a few more hours before I needed to be back to start up for the next day, but I didn't mind. I only had one more stop before getting home to a hot shower, reheated leftovers for dinner, and bed.

The ladies at the shelter and community center always looked at me like they were surprised to see me when I got there in the evenings, even though I visited several times a week. I handed Constance the basket, and Betty grabbed me by the sides of my face with her soft, grandmotherly hands and kissed my cheek.

"Such a sweet boy," she said like she always did.

I was well into my thirties and a foot taller than her, but Betty always described me in just that same way. I didn't mind it. She was the only one who could get away with it, but I didn't mind it coming from her.

"What can I do today?" I asked, looking around to see if I could catch sight of anything that needed to be done.

The center always had things that needed attention, and whether I was there for a short time in the evenings or for the full day I spent there once a month, I tried to do as much as I could. Constance, the younger of the two, would try to brush off my offer and say the food I brought was more than enough, but Betty was never one to turn down much-needed assistance.

I stayed at the center for another couple of hours before making my way home.

Chapter Three

Alexis

It was only a few days between signing my lease and getting the keys, but it felt like I was waiting forever. My excitement at finally getting the chance to move into the building I'd been coveting for so long had blinded me to the memory of the actual moving part of the equation. Somewhere along the lines, there was a disconnect, and I apparently thought I was just going to wake up already in the gorgeous apartment with everything organized for me.

That did not happen.

Instead, I woke up the morning of moving day with a sick feeling in my stomach and the hope that it was just jitters. I didn't have a lot of experience with moving. I'd grown up in the house where my father was born. Literally. It was a fast labor, and they didn't make it to the hospital. My grandmother didn't like to talk about it. The only times in my life I'd moved was when I went to college, and then when I moved into the old apartment I was moving out of and into the new one.

Those experiences hadn't been particularly good. Granted, the first one was marred by my family's disappointment and disapproving commentary because I had the gall to go to a university I chose for myself rather than my father's alma mater. I was also going to be living in student housing rather than either staying at home or moving into my own apartment nearby, so that wasn't going to go smoothly. And the second I ended up doing completely by myself because I was deeply rooted in my independence kick and thought I needed to be able to handle all challenges single-handedly.

That part of me was not familiar with the mechanics of one woman attempting to move a sectional sofa out of a tiny student apartment despite having aced physics.

This time I was determined not to make the experience that hard on myself. The notice was far too short to hire professional movers to do the entire move, so I did the next best thing. Or, more accurately, the only other option I had, and called in my friends. A crew was available to move the furniture from my old place as well as deliver a couple of new pieces I'd bought, but getting everything into the moving van and then into the new place was on us.

Which meant I spent the morning with Gabriela and her fiancé Dean talking about the wedding and all the plans that still needed to be finalized, Valerie waddling around being pregnant, and her husband Preston checking on her constantly and talking about pregnancy realities and baby preparations I really didn't need to hear coming from him. There are certain things women can talk about with their girlfriends and it's perfectly fine, but when it starts coming out of a man's mouth, it just goes to an icky place my china and throw pillows simply didn't need to be exposed to.

Even if I wasn't moving, this dynamic wouldn't have been my favorite. I loved my friends, but I always felt like the third—or fifth—wheel when they had their partners along. They were great guys, and I got along well with both of them, but when I was confronted with just how settled and coupled they were, it was nothing but a reminder that I was very single. I hadn't been looking for a relationship and was really determined to focus on my career and not get distracted by dating, but it still didn't feel great.

Fortunately, the guys only stayed around long enough to get everything off the moving truck and into the apartment. After a flurry of kisses and a sequence of check-ins, they left us with a mountain range of boxes to go through and not enough floor space available for the furniture that would be delivered eventually. *Eventually* being the operative and infuriating word there. The problem with that word was that it meant sometime in the future without any specification. I didn't work well with that. Especially considering the truck was supposed to have been at the new apartment almost an hour ago.

While the furniture not being there yet was working out for me in the sense that I didn't actually have anywhere to put it at the moment, it being late and not knowing when it might show up was just adding to my stress. This day was not turning out the way I'd envisioned.

"What do you think about this?"

I looked over to where Valerie was hanging a painting on the wall in the front hallway. Since she wasn't exactly in the condition to be hauling boxes or lifting anything of any real weight but still wanted to feel like she was playing some part in the whole process, she'd been assigned to hanging things and arranging pillows. I didn't have anything for her to arrange pillows on yet, so it had just been a lot of hammering so far. Hammering and talking about being hungry.

"It looks fine," I said.

"I am starving," she said. "Do we have any more of those nut packs?"

I thought I was being a prepared, responsible adult by packing a bag full of healthy snacks for the day with the obvious plan of ordering pizza as is tradition bestowed on the world by the gods of moving, but my planning was flawed. I hadn't taken into consideration the ravenous reality of a woman rapidly approaching the end of her third trimester. We'd already gone through all the snacks, had ordered a pizza, and were hotly debating what to have for dinner.

That was still a few hours away, though, and definitely after the furniture got there. But she'd mentioned being hungry every few minutes for the last hour, so I figured we weren't going to make it that long.

"We don't, but I'm going to get us something. You just keep on doing what you're doing. Looks great. Gabriela, keep trying to rearrange the boxes to make some sense of them and make room for the furniture whenever the hell it decides to get here. I'll be right back," I said.

"What are you going to get?" Valerie asked.

"I can't really go anywhere since we don't know when the truck is going to get here, so I'm just going to run down to the coffee shop in the lobby. I'm sure there are pastries. Maybe they even have some fruit cups or sandwiches or something. I'll just see what's available and maybe ask for some recommendations for takeout around here. How does that sound?" I asked.

"Perfect."

"Okay, good."

I left the apartment and went down into the lobby. I really didn't know what to expect from The Coffee Shop, but I hoped there was something good there. I wanted to thank my friends for being so willing to help me and for going out of their way for me. And I also just needed a bit of a pick-me-up to get through the rest of this mess of a day.

It wasn't until I'd gotten to the door of the shop that I remembered my glimpse of the sexy barista the day I came to look at the apartment. As soon as I walked inside, I saw him again, in the same place where he had been standing the first time. He had a bright, genuine smile on his face as he talked to a man dressed in three different types of plaid, and I felt a tug toward him.

I walked up to the counter and looked over the handwritten menu on the chalkboard behind it. There were a lot more options than I expected, but I wasn't sure what I should get.

"Hey, there," the man with the big smile said, stepping up in front of me. "What can I do for you?"

He was even more attractive not from a distance and not through glass, and for a second, I wasn't sure what I was supposed to say.

"I'm just moving in," I said when I'd gotten my thoughts back together and could think properly.

"Welcome," he said. "I hope you're settling in all right."

"Well, not exactly," I said. "I got the moving truck I filled with boxes and everything here, but the one with my furniture is MIA. I have two friends here helping me, and one of them is about three hundred months pregnant, so she's hungry. I wanted to grab a few things to eat to tide us through the afternoon."

"I can absolutely do that for you. My name is Nick," he said.

"I'm Alex."

"Well, Alex, do you have in mind what you want to order, or would you like me to put something together for you?" he asked.

He was so sweet and welcoming, and something about the smooth depth of his voice made my heart flutter. I couldn't let myself focus on that. But I couldn't turn down his offer of choosing the food. Usually, I resented people trying to make decisions for me, but with way this day was going and the number of things I already had going on in my mind, I was grateful for the break. Besides, he knew the menu and probably even knew what the mysterious "daily additions and specials" were. He'd made good decisions.

I watched him start to pull together an assortment of baked goods and then go into the open kitchen to make some sandwiches. He was talking as he did it, making sure none of us had any allergies or vehement food dislikes. He made sure there were no pregnancy food aversions to worry about and promised he would avoid the soft cheeses and meats that were warned against for pregnant women.

I was so wrapped up in watching him and listening to him, amazed at how courteous and considerate he was, I almost didn't pay attention to the movement out of the corner of my eye that said something was going on in front of the building. But it kept going, and when I looked up, I saw that it was the furniture delivery truck. Rather than going around to the back of the building to use the service entrance, they'd decided it was a good idea to just park in the middle of a busy city street.

"Shit shit shit," I muttered, getting up closer to the window and trying to gesture at the delivery driver to get his attention.

"Everything all right?" Nick asked.

"They showed up with the furniture, but they were supposed to bring it around back. They're blocking traffic, and I have a feeling the building owners won't be thrilled about me parading a bunch of furniture through the front lobby and attempting to stuff it in the elevator or drag it up the stairs," I said.

I knew for a fact they wouldn't be. Guidelines for moving in were very clearly outlined in the lease, including the required used of the back entrance and the strict restrictions on bringing in or out through the lobby anything from the apartment bigger than a standard box or suitcase. Everything else had to be moved through the service entrance that included a small loading dock and a freight elevator.

"Go ahead," Nick said. "Go talk to them. I'll finish getting your food together."

"Are you sure?" I asked.

"Absolutely. Go on."

"Thank you so much. Can you bring it up to my apartment? I don't know how much help they are going to give, and I don't particularly want them alone in my apartment with my friends," I said.

I knew I sounded a bit overprotective, but Nick didn't even flinch. He nodded, but then his face contorted slightly as if a realization stopped him.

"What's wrong?"

"I don't have the access code," Nick said. "I've never even been above the lobby."

"No worries," I said grabbing a napkin and a pen I saw sitting near the cash register. I jotted down the access code he would need to use to operate the elevator along with my apartment number.

Nick looked a little surprised, and I chastised myself as I ran outside to try to get the truck out of traffic and preserve the sanity of the entire block. I couldn't believe I'd just done that. This man was a complete stranger and yet I'd just given him access to the entire building.

Perfect.

Chapter Four

Nick

This had to be the woman Grayson had been talking about a few days before. There was only one apartment available in the building, which meant if she was moving in, she had to be the one he had given the tour to. I could absolutely see what he was talking about. She was gorgeous. Even if she did seem a bit frazzled. I couldn't blame her. Moving was very rarely an enjoyable experience, and when things weren't going according to plan, it could get really unpleasant, really fast.

This woman, Alex she'd said her name was, looked like she'd had just about enough, but by the way she was talking, there was still quite a bit to do. She was going to need plenty of fuel to keep her going, especially since she'd mentioned that one of the friends helping her was pregnant. I didn't have any children of my own, but I was far enough in age from my youngest siblings that I remembered my mother during her pregnancies, and two of my sisters had had babies in the last few years. If there was one thing I recalled about them during the last weeks was that they were constantly hungry. For good reason, though, so I was more than happy to make sure she had extra snacks and treats.

While Alex ran outside to flag down the truck driver and try to get him to go behind the building, I continued to gather the food for her. She'd essentially given me carte blanche to choose whatever I thought she'd enjoy, and I wanted to make sure she had plenty, but I also wanted to give her a friendly welcome to the building. I set out one of the baskets I keep around to pack special picnics and gifts my customers order and started filling it up.

As I worked on completing orders and filling her basket, I occasionally snuck glances out the window to watch her. I couldn't help but chuckle as she flailed around trying to get the guys to understand where she needed them to go and why stopping right there and hauling her furniture out onto the sidewalk wasn't going to work. I knew she was stressed and having a hard time, but she was also adorable. At one point she stopped, planting her hands on her hips and blowing a stream of air straight up at her forehead, making a wayward lock of hair that had escaped her already messy bun bounce up and out of the way.

Whether it was something she'd said or that single gesture, the truck crew seemed to finally understand what she needed from them and got back in the truck to head around the back of the building. Alex threw her arms up in the air in a gesture that seemed like a combination of exasperation and triumph, turned on her heel, and stalked down toward the alley at the side of the building. It would bring her to the back lot and the secured service entrance. The men would need a code to access the elevator, so there was nothing they could do until she got back there.

I finished preparing everything for her and looked over the basket I'd packed to see if there was anything I might have missed. I'd tried to include a wide variety, sweet and savory, different types of flavors, and several of the specialty items I offered to accommodate any dietary limitations she or her friends might have.

Sometimes it still surprised me when I put together baskets like this or looked at my email in the morning to find the inbox full of orders for picnics, birthday treats, and other special goods. When I first started planning The Coffee Shop, I didn't really envision the food being a very big part of the business. I thought I'd offer some pastries and basic baked goods to go along with the coffee and tea I thought would make up the majority of what people came in to get each day.

But as opening drew closer, the menu I was planning got more involved. Then after I opened, customers started mentioning things they were craving or thought would be good paired with my custom drinks or wrote in asking for things I didn't even offer, and I fell in love with baking. Now people come in for breakfast, lunch, and quick snacks just as much, if not even more, than cups of coffee.

Making the food had become one of my favorite parts of running the business, especially when I could do something special for one of my customers. I tried to acknowledge what they'd told me or things I knew about them with little treats and surprises, whether it was birthday cupcakes in their favorite flavor, heart-shaped sandwiches set aside for couples on their anniversary, or the peanut butter oat treats for Banana Split, I tried to give my regulars little bright spots in their days as much as I could. They didn't realize how much they did the same thing for me.

Just as I was adding wooden forks and spoons to the basket, Samuel, one of my employees, came in the door.

"Great. Perfect timing," I said as he came around the counter. "I have to run out for a second, but I'll be back in a few."

Samuel tied on his apron, eyeing the basket with a curious expression.

"Did someone make a special order?" he asked.

"Kind of," I told him. "The woman who is moving into the building today came to order some snacks for the people helping her, but she had to go deal with movers, so she asked me to bring it up."

"Ah, so that's what the people outside were complaining about. Apparently I just missed the truck being stopped directly in front of the building and completely blocking the entire street," Samuel said.

I laughed. "Yes, you did. It was definitely a choice on their part. And I think it pushed Alex right up to her limit. So I figured the least I can do is make sure she has something good to eat."

"Well, it looks like you've accomplished that," he said. "Go ahead. I'll hold down the fort."

"Thanks."

I grabbed the basket and went out into the lobby. It was a slightly strange experience walking farther into the building. I never went past The Coffee Shop. I rarely even went into the lobby. Usually, I entered through the door that led to the outside or through the private service entrance in the alley. I'd never gone into one of the elevators and definitely hadn't seen any of the apartments unless I counted seeing the shell of the building when it was still under construction and I was designing the shop space.

This was the perfect opportunity to indulge my curiosity, though, so I made sure to look around and take in everything around me as I walked across the lobby. When I got to the elevator, I typed in the code Alex had given me. Each resident of the building had a unique code that allowed access to the elevators as well as to the amenities such as the gym, spa, and entertainment rooms to ensure the security of the building.

The elevator doors opened, and I noticed it automatically selected the floor of Alex's apartment. It seemed like a good thought in theory, saving tenants having to select their own floor, but it did make me wonder what residents would do if they wanted to visit another floor. I had a feeling they would have to have fast fingers to hit another button before the elevator started moving.

The elevator shot upward, and the doors slid open to reveal a wide, brightly lit hallway. A mirror set directly in front of the elevator showed me standing there with the basket, and I realized I was still wearing my work apron. I was strangely embarrassed by it and didn't quite understand why. Alex had just seen me in the shop wearing it, and it wasn't like she didn't know I was delivering them to her. Or like this was a social call. I wasn't just swinging by to see her, so the apron really shouldn't matter. I still considered taking it off before getting to the door but changed my mind as I walked down the hall toward her apartment door.

The door to the apartment was closed, and I listened for a few seconds. I could hear voices inside, so I knocked. There was some shuffling inside and a couple of muffled profanities before the door opened. A woman that was decidedly not Alex stared out at me. She made no effort to cover up the fact that she was looking me up and down, taking me in like I had the lobby.

"Hello," she said.

There was something in that word that was more than just a greeting, but I wasn't going to acknowledge it.

"Hi," I said. "I'm Nick."

I figured this was one of the friends Alex told me was helping her move and she hadn't told them I would be coming up. No flicker of recognition seemed to register across her eyes. Maybe Alex hadn't said anything.

"Hi, Nick," she said. She looked me up and down again. "Gotta love a man in an apron."

Maybe I should have gone with taking off the apron.

"Is Alex here? I have this for her," I said.

"She isn't in right now. But she sure did pick a good building. She has such sweet new neighbors bringing goodies," the woman said.

There was a salacious note in her voice, but the way she was leaning on the door frame showed off her very large engagement ring.

"Um, actually, I'm not her neighbor," I started to clarify, but the sound of metal at the end of the hallway stopped me.

I looked down to where the hallway turned and saw Alex coming around it backward, gesturing like she was trying to bring a plane in for landing. A second later, a large piece of furniture followed her around the corner.

"There she is," the woman said. "Hey, Alex. A cupcake showed up at the door. And he brought treats."

Oh, lord.

Chapter Five

Alexis

Oh, crap.

Gabriela had gotten to Nick. I'd hoped I would get back up to the apartment before he got there and be able to cut her off at the pass, but it hadn't worked out that way. It turned out negotiating a sectional into a service elevator wasn't quite as easy as I envisioned. Now he'd walked right into her sticky gaze.

I loved Gabriela. She was my oldest friend, and we'd been through it all together. I also knew she wouldn't cheat on Dean, who she absolutely adored and had devoted herself to over the last three years. At least, I hoped she wouldn't. I really didn't think she would. But she had always been a tremendous flirt. It was just part of her being as a human. No matter what the situation or her current status, if she got to within a hundred yards of a man she found attractive, something just clicked in her, and she went full-on sultry femme fatale.

I liked to tease that she was going to grow up to be one of those cougar women who wore animal print spandex pants and stilettos while hitting on men young enough to be their grandsons. To my credit, Gabriela had never once denied this possibility. I figured Dean would just be along for the ride, holding her purse and shaking his head.

Hoping the furniture guys could manage to get the piece the rest of the way to my apartment without my navigation, I rushed down the hall to save Nick.

"Hey," I said. "Gabriela, this is Nick."

"We met," Gabriela said in a way that I could really only describe as purring as much as it pained me to even apply that word.

"Well, kind of," Nick said.

"Nick, this is Gabriela, my oldest and best friend, and a glowing bride-to-be," I introduced. Gabriela visibly pouted, and I had to bite my bottom lip to stop myself from laughing. "Gabriela, this is Nick. He works at The Coffee Shop downstairs. He was nice enough to take my order and bring the food up to us so I could talk to the furniture guys."

"That was nice of him," Gabriela said. "I didn't realize you were moving into such a hospitable building, Alex. Maybe there are other services Nick could help you out with."

"Gabriela," I warned, "stop it." I looked at the basket Nick was still holding. "This looks absolutely incredible. Thank you so much."

I saw a few of the things I'd seen on the menu along with tons of other sweets and surprises.

"Consider it a welcome to the building," he said.

"You didn't have to do that," I said.

"I know," he said. "But I wanted to."

"Thank you. It's really amazing."

I took the basket, and almost immediately the sectional showed up behind me and I got pushed out of the way and into Nick. He caught me by my upper arms and held me in place for a brief second. The basket kept our bodies from pressing against each other, and I had the fleeting thought that I'd never been so upset at a muffin before.

"Where do you want this thing?" one of the delivery guys asked, his voice muffled from his face being nearly buried in the fabric of the furniture. They probably should have considered having a third man on the job, but I was the woman who'd spent three and a half hours moving it by myself, so what did I know?

"In the living room," I said, stepping out of the way. I looked up at Nick apologetically. "I'm sorry. I've got to deal with this whole situation."

What I really wanted to do was to stop and talk to him, but I really didn't have the time. I needed to make sure the furniture actually got into my apartment and into the right places. I didn't have a ton of faith in this particular moving team and was starting to really understand why they were available at such short notice. I had the feeling if I just stayed out of the way I was going to end up with parts of different pieces of furniture in various rooms, my bed in the living room, and my dresser in the kitchen.

"No, don't apologize. Go ahead. I understand," Nick said. He reached for the basket and took it out of my hands. "Here, let me bring this in for you. I'll just put it on the dining table. Does that work?"

"Well, the dining table is still in the truck, so that might not be the best choice," I said.

He gave a single nod, cringing slightly. "Right. That's the whole point of this, isn't it? Well, is there a kitchen counter currently in proper position inside the apartment?"

"Yes. I do have one of those," I said.

"Great. I'll put it there," he said.

"Perfect."

The sectional was out of the way enough for us to go inside, and I directed him toward the kitchen. He set the basket and the drink container down and unloaded the drinks.

"There's sugar and cream in the basket for the coffee," he said when I walked in behind him. "If there are any flavors or anything you might like, just let me know. I can get it up to you."

"You've already done way more than enough," I said. "Thank you so much for doing all this. What do I owe you?"

Nick waved his hand through the air, brushing me off. "Don't worry about it. Like I said, it's a welcome to the building."

"I can't do that," I said, shaking my head.

"Of course, you can. I insist."

"At least let me offer you something to thank you for going out of your way to come up here and bring it to me. You had to leave your shift and everything," I said.

Nick seemed to fight a little bit of a smile curling his lips. "It wasn't my shift."

"Oh. Oh, no. Did I come in there when you were already off for the day and get you to do all this?" I asked, feeling embarrassed.

"No. I mean, I don't work at The Coffee Shop. I own it," Nick said.

And now I wanted to crawl into a hole and seal it up with a sectional cushion.

"Of course, you do," I said. "I'm sorry. I didn't..."

Nick shook his head, allowing himself a full smile now. "It's fine. Don't worry about it. I just didn't want you to think my boss was going to be mad at me or anything."

I groaned and put my face in my hand. "Just firing on all cylinders making good impressions over here."

Nick laughed. "I think you made a great impression."

My heart fluttered again as our eyes met for a second. A loud, ominous thump in the front of the apartment broke the feeling, and I let out a sigh.

"That didn't sound good."

We rushed toward the sound and found one of my tables on its side and a large chair on its back. I didn't know how that happened, and I didn't really want to know how it happened. I just wanted this whole process to be over and for nothing else to get dropped.

"Sorry," one of the movers said. "Your stuff is really heavy."

I was tempted to ask him if he was accustomed to moving doll-house furniture or if he operated solely in the cardboard cutout market, but I stopped myself. Nick already talking also helped.

"Why don't you let me help you out a little?" he said. "We'll get the stuff up here faster."

"No," I said, shaking my head. "No, Nick. You've already done enough. I can't ask you to be a moving man, too."

"Furniture moving specialist," one of the guys corrected.

I slid my eyes over to him, and Nick moved just enough to keep my focus on him.

"You're not asking me. I'm offering. And it would just make this whole experience easier. Think of it this way. You were just talking about making impressions. I bet your neighbors wouldn't love listening to more furniture being dropped," he said.

"That's true," I said.

"Good. All right, guys, let's go."

He headed out of the apartment, and I looked over at Gabriela. She looked over at me with an open mouth.

"Holy Hotcakes," she mouthed.

I rolled my eyes. "Nope."

I walked out of the apartment and made my way down the steps rather than going the way of the service elevator. Having already done the trip in that thing once, I knew it wasn't spacious. I preferred not to get that cozy with the guys again if I could avoid it.

For the next half an hour, Nick helped unload the rest of the furniture and bring it into the apartment. When the last piece was at least semi-in place in the correct room, he told me he was going to head back down to his shop. I thanked him again, wishing there was something else I could do or say to show my appreciation, but he just smiled and disappeared.

Gabriela was on me the second the door closed.

"Holy hell, that guy is hot."

"You're engaged, Gabriela. Your wedding is in less than a month," I pointed out.

"I'm aware of that. But that doesn't mean I don't have fully functioning eyes. You can't just pretend you didn't notice how sexy he is," she said.

I gave a non-committal half shrug. "Yeah, I mean, I guess he was pretty good looking."

Her mouth fell open. "You have got to be kidding me."

"What does she have to be kidding you about?" Valerie asked, yawning as she came into the room.

She'd fallen asleep while I was downstairs ordering the food and playing traffic cop for the furniture truck and had managed to stay asleep through all of the chaos and uproar of the furniture coming into the apartment. Pregnancy hormones were no joke.

"Oh, you missed it," Gabriela said. "This sexy as hell guy from the coffee shop downstairs brought up a huge basket of muffins and sandwiches and stuff. But seriously, he was the snack."

I rolled my eyes. "Did you really just refer to a grown-ass male adult as a 'snack'? How old are you?"

"I stand by it," Gabriela said. "And don't try to deflect. That guy was gorgeous. And he was obviously interested in you."

"No, he wasn't. He just wanted to be friendly and welcome me to the building," I said.

"The man brought you an overflowing picnic basket of goodies and then stayed and moved furniture for you. That is not any kind of welcoming committee I know about," she said.

"It was very nice of him," I admitted. "But that's it. I think he's just that kind of guy. I mean, there was this customer sitting at the shop just rambling on and on, and Nick stood there and talked to him and laughed. I think he's just friendly. I know that's a big shock to the system that there might be good guys in the world, but they do exist."

"I know they do. That's why I'm marrying one of them," Gabriela said.

"So you shouldn't be worrying yourself with whether or not Nick is one of them," I said.

"Again, not for me. For you. You are not marrying one of them. You are not even breathing near any of them at any point. When was the last time you went on a date?"

"I don't have time to talk about this," I said. "Just like I don't have time to even think about dating. There's far too much going on in my life right now to even consider trying to deal with anything like that."

"I'm just bummed I missed him," Valerie said as she carried a massive chocolate chip muffin out of the kitchen. "You guys get all the good stuff."

"Says the pregnant woman," I pointed out.

We all laughed, and I went into the kitchen to grab a snack for myself. Gabriela was still talking about Nick in the other room, insisting she thought I should go for him, but I wasn't going to acknowledge it anymore. I'd literally spoken to the man on this one day. And he worked in my building. It would just be too strange trying to work around all of that.

But just between me and the orange biscuits, it was a nice thought.

Chapter Six

Nick

The next day hit the ground running. That happened sometimes. There wasn't any particular rhyme or reason to it, but there were certain days when the crowds seemed to be more caffeine-starved than others and there would be a constant stream of customers from the moment I opened the door.

That day was one of those days, with a couple people standing outside the door before I even opened it. They looked impatient and antsy, like they thought if they didn't get their hands on coffee and a cream cheese pastry soon, they were going to collapse right there in the lobby or on the city sidewalk. Being the humanitarian that I am, I didn't want to see that happen on my account, so I got through my early morning preparations as quickly as I could and opened up a few minutes earlier than I usually did.

As soon as we were open, I was busy, and I was glad to see Kristie show up for her shift. She was the second of my two employees, and the one I usually relied on to help me over the hump on busy mornings. There was almost always a crush first thing with people getting fueled up for the day ahead of them or possibly picking up treats for the office or placing special orders for later in the day. There was rarely a time when the shop was completely empty, but after the first couple of very busy hours, I could generally breathe for a few minutes at least.

I was hoping it was going to be during one of those calmer minutes that Alex came in. She'd been eager to drink the coffee I brought her when she moved in, so I thought maybe she would make the shop a stop on her regular pass through the lobby.

As it turned out, I was right about her wanting to stop by and get coffee. But I was wrong about the timing. I was busy filling a complicated coffee order and helping a customer select between a few different flavors of muffins when I caught sight of her out of the corner of my eye. She rushed in like she was on a mission and jumped into the line. She was looking at the phone in her hand, occasionally typing furiously, and didn't look up until she was already standing at the counter with Kristie helping her.

I turned around to give the customer in front of me her blueberry lemon poppyseed muffin, and when I turned back around, Alex was already hightailing it for the door again. It felt strange to be so disappointed that I wasn't able to talk to her. I didn't even know her, but I wanted to. I hadn't felt that way in what felt like a long time. But I couldn't waste too much time thinking about it. I had to focus on work, and that day seemed like one that was going to take every bit of my energy and concentration to handle.

Barry hadn't come in the day before, which was unusual for him, so when he walked through the door at the very end of the morning rush, I flashed him a wide smile.

"Hey, Barry," I said. "How're you doing today?"

"Tired," he told me, dropping down onto his regular stool with a deep exhale and a dropped his shoulders like he needed to physically demonstrate what he was feeling in addition to telling me. "I was up with Banana Split all night."

"Oh, no," I said, going to work putting together his regular order. "Is there something wrong?"

"He had to get all his puppy shots yesterday, and it was very rough. They made him go back into the back without me for his weigh-in and to get his nails clipped, and then they gave him all his shots and poked and prodded him. He's just a baby. I don't know why they needed to do all that to him," he said.

His voice was getting tense with emotion. He was clearly already deeply bonded to this little dog.

"They were just doing what's best for him," I reassured him. "I know it's tough to watch him go through that, but he's going to be healthier for it."

"I know. But he seemed so pitiful when it was over, like he just couldn't understand why I would let them do all that to him. It broke my heart. And then he was whimpery and lethargic the rest of the day. I thought he had a fever, and I called the emergency vet line, but they said he was going to be fine. They didn't even see him, so I don't know why they would think they knew that. I stayed up with him and gave him warm milk and snacks throughout the night and held him when he was sleeping to make sure he was going to be okay."

"How is he doing this morning?" I asked.

"Much better. He wanted to take a walk, and he chased a butterfly. It was so good to see him back to his normal self," Barry said.

I chuckled to myself, appreciating how secure he was in his evaluation of his puppy's normal self when he had only known him a couple of days. But he was attached and devoted, and that's really all a dog can hope for in life, so I was happy for both of them.

"Well, good. I'm glad to hear it. And because he's feeling better, maybe he'll be up for a special treat when you get home?" I asked.

I went into the back to where I'd stored the bone-shaped peanut butter oat cookies and brought them out to Barry. He was as thrilled as I expected, and as soon as I told him they were human grade, he had to try one, also as I expected. He was doing the contemporary equivalent of showing a wallet full of pictures of the puppy by scrolling through a folder in his phone when I felt a light tap on the back of my shoulder. I turned to Kristie.

"Hey," I said. "You done for the day?"

"Yes, but I wanted to tell you there's someone who wants to talk to you," she said.

I did my best not to show it, but I felt a little spark when she said that. Maybe Alex had run out on a fast errand, but then came back to talk to me. I nodded.

"Where?" I asked.

She pointed behind her toward a cluster of furniture in the corner. I took off my apron and was trying to control the smile I could feel tugging on my cheeks as I walked toward the end of the counter. The smile went away and was replaced with a feeling of being a completely ridiculous schoolboy when I realized Alex was not sitting on the couch or any of the overstuffed chairs. She wasn't even standing near the more near one of the few tables I had arranged I give people a place to sit if I wanted to stay in the shop, about the stools at the counter were full.

Instead, I saw that the person sitting on the couch was a man in a sharp suit talking on the phone and flipping through something on his tablet while still managing to look bored. Which meant I knew exactly why he was there. I dealt with a couple of people just like him every month. In fact, I was fairly certain I'd seen this particular man at least once. Whether or not he was going to acknowledge that or try to pretend like this was the first time he was approaching me was yet to be seen.

I walked up to the coffee table in front of the couch and waited for a second to see if he was paying enough attention to realize I was standing there. I wanted to see how much he was actually invested in this meeting. Falling right in line with what I thought, he just kept right on with his phone call and his tablet. This was just another in what was probably a long list of appointments he had scheduled for the day. It was at once frustrating and refreshing.

Frustrating because if he was going to come into the business I'd worked so hard to build and try to get me to sell it to him, which I knew was exactly what he was going to say when he noticed me and started talking, the least he could do was make it seem like he had actual interest.

Refreshing because at least this time I wasn't on the receiving end of a saccharine stream of over-enthusiasm from someone who thought if they made me feel like I was some visionary genius who'd created the concept of the coffee shop I'd be manipulated into selling, or at the very least, franchising.

"You wanted to speak with me?" I finally said after reaching the end of my patience for how long I was willing to just stand there waiting for him.

The man looked up and nodded, taking another several seconds to bring his phone call to a close before standing up and extending a hand toward me.

"Nick, it's good to see you again," he said in a booming voice.

So much for him being genuine. I'd never told him it was okay to refer to me by my first name, and since the only interactions we'd had before this moment amounted to approximately five minutes of conversation a month before, I had significant doubts he was actually feeling any sense of happiness about being here. Unless we were currently embroiled in some sort of strange slow-burn friendship, I didn't think anything was coming from this.

"Hello," I said. "I really do need to get back to work, so what would you like to speak to me about?"

I was doing my best to remain polite while also giving him as little space as I could to embark on his likely planned spiel. He looked somewhat taken aback but continued on anyway.

"I was in the area and thought I'd stop by and see if you had thought any more about my proposition," he said.

"As we already discussed, I am not interested in selling my business. There's nothing I need to think about more or reconsider," I said.

Just then, Grayson walked in. For once, I was glad about his arrival.

"Nick, I really think if you would just…"

"I'm sorry," I said, stepping back from him, "someone just came in. I'll need to end this conversation. Thanks for stopping in, though. Have a great afternoon."

I went back behind the counter, and Grayson came up, his eyes flashing back and forth between me and the man whose name I couldn't remember and who hadn't bothered to re-introduce himself. He was probably accustomed to being extremely memorable.

"What's that all about?" he asked.

"Nothing," I said. "Just another investment company wanting to buy The Coffee Shop and turn it corporate."

"You're not going to do that, are you?" Grayson asked.

"No. And that's exactly what I told him. This time and the last time he came in."

Grayson laughed. "Good. So I just found out another apartment is coming open next month."

"Oh?" I asked.

"Yeah. Turns out one of the guys who bought in at the beginning is divorcing his second wife, and the settlement included selling it and giving her half."

He looked like he thought this was hilarious.

"I guess that means you're going to be plucking another lucky name off the waitlist," I said, not wanting to encourage his gossiping.

"Yep. I'm making the first call this afternoon. Hopefully it will be another woman and as hot as the last one. It would be nice to have some options." He glanced to the side, and I saw a lascivious look cross his face. "Speak of the devil."

I followed his gaze and saw Alex walking in. She looked up at me and smiled. Grayson stepped out of the way, but as soon as Alex came up to me, he stepped behind her. His frat boy energy took over, and he started making faces and gestures toward her. I glared at him, trying to get him to understand I wanted him to stop, but he kept going.

"Hey," Alex said. "How are you?"

"I'm good," I said. "It's been a busy day. I'm ready for everybody to leave so I can be done."

Grayson took the hint and gave me a salute before starting out, but Alex had also thought the comment was directed to her, and her cheeks went pink. It would have been charming if I didn't know it was because she was embarrassed.

"Oh," she said. "I'm sorry, I can come back tomorrow."

"No," I said, probably a bit too quickly. "No, I didn't mean you. I'm glad you're here."

I wasn't really intending for that part to come out, but she was gracious enough to not comment on it. Instead, she looked down, and I realized she had her hands behind her back.

"Well, I came by this morning, but it was crazy busy, so I didn't get a chance to see you. I wanted to thank you again for everything you did for me yesterday. I really appreciate your help. I don't think that the furniture would even be in my apartment right now if it wasn't for you. I'd be sleeping somewhere between the back alleyway and the hall where they would have left my bed."

I laughed. "I don't know if it was that dire, but it was my pleasure. I'm glad I could make moving in a little easier for you."

"You made it a lot easier for me. Including making sure we didn't starve. That basket you brought was so incredible with all the wonderful treats, and since you mentioned some of them were your special favorites, I thought I would bring you something was really special to me when I was a child and that gives me a lot of happy memories."

Her hands came from around her back, and she presented me with a plate of lemon bars, plastic wrap pulled tightly over the top. I was touched by the gesture, especially considering lemon bars had been one of my favorite desserts since I was a small child.

"Thank you," I said. "I love lemon bars." I glanced around and saw that the shop had emptied out. It was just the two of us. "Care to join me for one?"

She nodded. "I'd love to."

I made each of us a cup of coffee and brought them over to where Alex was sitting on the same couch the businessman had vacated. I set the cups on the table beside the plate and peeled the plastic back. Some of the powdered sugar went with it, and I remembered how many times my grandmother's kitchen was coated in sugar after she made a batch.

Each of us picked up one of the bars. I was impressed at how perfect they looked, and when I inhaled the scent of them, more memories came flooding back. I took a bite, and something tickled the back of my mind.

"Do you like it?" she asked.

"I do," I said. "Something tastes really familiar. Did you put turmeric in these?"

Her face went blank. She looked down at the lemon bar in her hand and opened her mouth like she was going to answer, then closed it. Her eyes lifted back up to mine.

"I didn't make these," she finally admitted. "I bought them."

I laughed. "Where did you get them?"

"A little gift boutique not too far from here," she said, cringing as she set the rest of her bar down on a napkin. "Gabriela, you remember her..."

"Vividly."

"Yeah. That's Gabriela. She and I were out shopping today for some last things to put in the welcome bags for her out-of-town wedding guests, and we ended up at that little shop. I saw these bars, and they looked delicious, and I really did enjoy lemon bars when I was a child, so I bought them."

Alex let out a sigh. I laughed again.

"I made them."

Her eyes went wide. "What?"

"I baked these. I know the boutique you're talking about. I have an arrangement with the owner. I bring baked goods in there a couple of times a week," I said. I took another bite. "So yes, there is turmeric in them. Don't tell anybody."

Chapter Seven

Alexis

I wanted to crawl under the couch and die right then. I was completely humiliated. I could not believe this was happening. Of all the places in this city I could have gone and bought something sweet to give him as a thank you, I had to go into that one. All I wanted to do was show my appreciation—and maybe have another excuse to spend some time with him—and I'd managed to present him with lemon bars he had baked his damn self.

This was quite possibly one of the most cringeworthy moments of my life, but Nick wasn't acting how I would have expected a man to in his situation. He didn't make fun of me or try to make me feel small, or worse, act offended that I'd done something just on this side of shady. Instead, he was sweet and jovial, laughing, but also eating his lemon bar with abandon. I decided if he wasn't going to turn it into something negative, neither would I. At least, not outwardly.

I picked my lemon bar up again and took another bite.

"You know," I said, examining the bar and its wonderful flurry of powdered sugar on top, "I just want to point out that I didn't actually say I made these. I just said they were some of my favorites. And in my defense, they are exactly like the ones from my childhood. Baked by someone who isn't in my family." We both laughed, and I shrugged. "It's true. Every woman in my family is a terrible baker."

"Really?" Nick asked.

"Oh, for sure. Like epic levels of incompetence around ovens. But my mother always wanted to be the picture perfect housewife and mother, and that meant that she had to have fabulous baked goods available. So she would buy things and fake them all the time. Like literally take brownies out of bakery boxes, put them in a baking pan, and smoosh them around a little so it looked like they had been baked in there. Sometimes she would even put canned icing on them so it didn't look like they'd been cut already."

Nick laughed harder. I enjoyed the sound. It was rich and rolling, a genuine sound rather than something forced or clipped like so often happened.

"Well, thank you, anyway," he said. "I haven't actually eaten a lemon bar in..."

"A few hours since you baked these?" I asked, laughing over the words.

He shrugged again. "Maybe."

"At least I know you like them. So thank you, again."

"Of course. How are you settling in?"

"It's coming along," I said. "I mean, it's still really new, and I'm surrounded by boxes, but I know where to find my pillows, towels, and TV remote, so as long as there are restaurants around, I'm pretty good."

"It's hard to get used to a new place," Nick said.

"It definitely is. And right now was probably not the wisest choice in terms of timing. I'm already so busy with work, plus my best friend is getting married and I am the maid of honor, and my other best friend is getting ready to have her first baby, so there's all kinds of things happening with that. It's just a lot and I've been a bit busy. But hopefully, I will get a chance to make it feel more like home soon."

"The best friend getting married is Gabriela?" Nick asked. "The one I met?"

"The one who hit on you shamelessly?" I asked. "Yeah, that would be the one. But don't worry, she's harmless. Flirting incessantly is kind of her language."

He nodded. "Well, she is fluent, I'll give her that. I think she was secretly hoping I was going to ask to borrow a cup of sugar."

A ripple of heat went up the back of my neck and across my cheeks, but I willed it to go away and covered it as best I could by finishing up the lemon bar.

"So do you live in the building?" I asked.

Nick shook his head. "No. I don't live too far from here, though. I usually walk unless the weather is really bad. I managed to get in when the building was still under development and no other businesses had shown interest. I was really lucky to snag the spot."

"It's pretty perfect," I said. "Having good coffee this close to home is kind of a dream."

"Does your family have difficulty brewing coffee as well?" he asked, managing to keep a completely straight face until I glared at him.

"Hilarious. But ... I mean, kind of." He laughed again, and I shrugged like he had. "I mean, I can use one of those single-cup brewer things, but that's about the extent of my wizardry. It gets me by. But I much prefer the kinds of things you make here. And I definitely don't have a revolving selection of pastries in my kitchen, so that's another plus in your column."

"Come by again soon and see what's rotated in," Nick said.

My heart thumped a little in my chest. "Maybe I will."

I walked out of the shop and started across the lobby. Almost as soon as I did, I saw the guy who had given me the tour of my apartment coming toward me with the same wide grin on his face. Only this time, there was something behind the look in his eyes that wasn't the hope I was going to sign a lease. I'd felt the player vibe coming off him when he gave me the tour, and I wasn't too keen on dealing with more of it.

"Hey, you," he said. He was definitely that type. He didn't even remember my name. "It's so nice to see you again. I was hoping I'd run into you."

"Hi, Grayson," I said but didn't stop my progress toward the elevator.

"Coming from The Coffee Shop?" he asked even though I was positive he'd seen me walk out.

"Yes," I said.

"It's a great place. Our residents really appreciate it. It's one of the services the Bentley is proud to offer to make living here as comfortable and enjoyable as possible," he said.

There was so much smug pride in his voice it made my skin crawl. He was still following me, and I was strongly considering turning around and leaving the building just to see if he was perhaps like a ghost and couldn't leave the perimeter. But my luck would be he would just think I wanted to have a nice walk with him and come right along. So instead, I gave him a questioning look.

"Really? I had no idea the Bentley owned The Coffee Shop. I thought that was Nick."

Grayson looked shocked, like he certainly wasn't expecting that. He stuttered for a second, then rebounded with another of his well-rehearsed smiles.

"Well, yes. Nick does own it. What I meant was the Bentley is extremely selective in the businesses permitted in the building, and Nick was very fortunate to be chosen as the coffee option provided for the residents," he said.

"So it was the idea of the company that owns the building to have a coffee shop in the lobby?" I asked. "Because Nick told me he got into the spot while the building was still under development and other businesses hadn't even been considered."

I don't say it with any accusation, instead employing a soft tone of affected confusion to make him feel small and uneasy. He knew he'd been caught.

"The shop is a fantastic asset," he said with a note at the end of his voice that sounded like he was bringing that portion of the conversation to a tidy close. I had to try not to laugh.

We got to the elevator, and Grayson paused, waiting for me to put in my code to activate the doors. I didn't, but he didn't move.

"I'm going to go ahead and go up now," I said. "Thanks for saying hello."

"I bet the apartment looks great now that you've had a chance to put your own touches to it," he said.

"It's coming along," I said. "There's still unpacking and settling in to do."

"Of course. That takes some time. But still. The last time I saw it, it was empty. And before that, it was still full of all the old tenant's stuff. It probably seems like a totally different place with you there."

It was obvious he was angling for an invitation to come up and see what I'd done with the apartment, but that was so far from not happening it wasn't even in the realm of reality.

"I think every place looks different when different people move into it," I pointed out.

He let out a polite, fake laugh, the kind that made Nick's so wonderful.

"True. I would love to see how you made it your own," he said. "I'm sure you have amazing taste."

I stopped myself short of pointing out that my taste was what was going to keep me from letting him into the elevator with me. Instead, I stared him directly in the eyes.

"I have to wash my hair."

I turned back around and typed my code into the keypad, feeling like there were different words I was actually supposed to say in that space, but those were the ones that actually came out. Whatever was supposed to be there, it didn't really matter because Grayson seemed to get the message. He didn't try to follow me into the elevator when the doors opened. He didn't wave back at me when I waved at him as they closed, either.

Even though Grayson hadn't made any moves to accompany me up, I still gave a good faith pause and checked around the corners and the door to the stairwell before heading for my apartment door. I didn't feel intimidated by him or threatened in any way. He was annoying, not scary. And I had a feeling he was going to get over his amusement soon. He was the kind of guy who got entranced by a new, shiny thing and was easily distracted by the next one when it came along. I just had to wait it out. He'd get bored soon enough.

I got into my apartment and changed into comfortable clothes before settling in front of my laptop. I pulled up a search for how to make lemon bars. It seriously could not be that difficult. I needed to add at least one recipe into my assortment of skills in case of a baked good emergency.

A few minutes later, my phone rang.

"Hey, Valerie," I answered.

"Are you busy?" she asked.

"Nope. Just doing some research."

"Research about what?" she asked.

"Lemon juice versus lemon extract," I said. "Why? What's up?"

"Could you come over?"

"Is everything all right? Are you okay?"

It was still several weeks before the baby was supposed to come, but I was already on high alert. Gabriela had made it one of my sworn maid of honor duties to ensure the baby didn't make his grand appearance at the wedding. Before was also greatly frowned upon. After they returned from their honeymoon was the preferred option.

"Yeah, I'm fine. Preston just left for a business trip this morning, and now I'm lonely. Can you just come over and keep me company for a little while?" she asked.

"All right. I'm on my way."

"Thank you. Have you had dinner? I'll order Thai," she said.

It was all one thought. I didn't have a say in it.

As I was leaving the building, I saw Nick coming out of the front door of his shop and locking up. It had started to rain a little, and he pulled the collar of his jacket up over the back of his neck.

"Hey, Nick," I called after him.

He turned around and smiled.

"Good night, Alex," he said.

He turned and started walking down the sidewalk like he told me he usually did.

"It's raining," I said. "Can I give you a ride?"

He turned around and shook his head with a smile. "I'll be fine. It's just a few blocks. Thank you, though. Have a good night."

"You, too."

Sometime between my apartment and me actually getting to Valerie's place, the Thai food order changed to Thai food, Indian food, a pizza, some beef jerky, three different flavors of slushies, ice cream, and Doritos. It was a questionable assortment even without being mixed together, which Valerie was doing in some very concerning combinations. She said it was what the baby wanted, so I didn't question it. I avoided it with everything in me, but I didn't question it.

While I sat and ate my very basic bowl of peanut noodles, we talked about her other cravings, her current pregnancy symptoms, her worries about labor, and impending motherhood. As she talked about it, I wondered not for the first time if this was something in my future. I hadn't yet decided if I wanted to be a mother. I figured I had some time. Not having a partner added to that time significantly.

Chapter Eight

Nick

Early the next morning, I was filling the display case with the day's offering of pastries, muffins, biscuits, and other baked goods when I glanced up and caught sight of Alex running through the lobby. She wasn't running toward the doors like she was rushing to get somewhere. Instead, she was running from off the street for the elevator, wearing what looked like the same thing she had been in the night before.

I went to the door leading into the lobby, and when she stopped at the elevator to put her code in, I called out to her.

"Good morning, Alex. Everything okay?"

She looked back over her shoulder and nodded, but there was a distinct sense of urgency in the gesture and in the way she was bouncing on her feet while waiting for the elevator to open. I noticed sometimes the elevators tended to be slower first thing in the morning, almost like they were tired, too, and needed a little bit of time to warm up before they could go at full speed. More likely it was because there were a lot more people moving around between floors.

"I fell asleep at Valerie's house last night without meaning to, and now I have to get ready and not be late for work," she said.

The elevator doors opened, and she ducked into them, waving as they closed. I went back into the shop and began making a cup of the same coffee she had ordered the day before. While it was brewing, I packed a paper bag with a fresh breakfast sandwich and a pastry along with some napkins. With everything ready, I stepped outside the door and waited in the lobby.

It didn't take long for the elevator doors to open back up and Alex to come running out again. She had made what struck me as a fairly miraculous transformation in the only short length of time she was up in her apartment. Somehow in just a little more than the time it took me to brew coffee and pack some breakfast items, she had managed to go from having slept in her clothes to being polished and put together for a day at the office.

"I'm impressed," I said as she approached.

She gave me an acknowledging look and nodded. "Yeah, I have more experience than I'd like to admit having to throw myself together at the last second. I have the dubious skill of being able to fall asleep just about anywhere and in any context, and friends that don't bother to wake me even when I really should be woken up," she said. "Have a good day."

"Wait," I said, holding out the coffee and breakfast. "You're probably going to need some extra caffeine this morning once all that adrenaline leaves you. And you can't go to work without breakfast. I didn't know if you would be in the mood for something savory or something sweet, so there's a sandwich with egg, cheese, and bacon, and then there's a pastry."

She looked happy as she took the bag from me.

"Thank you so much. You are a lifesaver," she said.

"Have a good day."

She was already sipping the coffee on her way out the door, and I had to laugh. I was learning new things about her every time I saw her, and I was enjoying every one of them.

When I ducked back into the shop, I saw that a small group of customers had come in off the street and were standing just inside, looking around and seeming both confused and concerned. I smiled at them as I crossed to behind the counter to start my day.

Kristie showed up a few minutes later, and with her seemingly came the rest of the morning rush. I didn't have much time to think about Alex as I kept up with the customers and took special orders. It seemed the beautiful weather forecast for the next few days had inspired a lot of romantic picnics and generous moods from bosses who wanted to bring snacks and treats for their offices.

The day hadn't started off too busy, but the crowd was thick and steady, and even when it was time for Kristie to leave so she could get to her college classes on time, there was still a dense crowd. She looked at me apologetically, but I brushed her out the door. She wasn't going to miss class just so people didn't have to wait a few extra moments for their coffee.

That crowd carried me right through to the early afternoon, when it dissipated just in time for Grayson to come swaggering in. Apparently he had decided to make my shop his regular spot. I wasn't sure when we had become such good friends, but I was going to have to look out for things like that more in the future.

This time, he wasn't alone. A blond woman was hanging on him like she wasn't fully confident in her ability to support her own body weight on long, predominantly bare legs. She looked like she was also probably wearing the same thing she had the night before, but I thought it was doubtful it was because she'd accidentally fallen asleep somewhere.

"Morning, Nick," Grayson said with a big grin.

I glanced at the old-fashioned clock positioned in the middle of the main wall. Just confirming I hadn't imagined a couple of hours go by.

"Afternoon, Grayson," I said. "Taking a lunch break?"

The woman laughed like it was the funniest thing she'd heard in a long time, the exertion making her body swing so Grayson had to hold on to her waist more tightly to keep her on her feet.

"Actually, just getting started. I have the day off, so I thought I'd reward myself with sleeping in a bit."

He waggled his eyebrows at me as if I needed something else to get the not-so-hidden message behind that comment through my head.

I nodded. "Sounds good. Can I get you something?"

A buzzing sound from somewhere in the vicinity of the blond woman made her face pucker like she'd sucked a lemon. She reached down into her cleavage and pulled out a tiny cell phone. Looking at the screen, she let out a sigh, her shoulders dropping and her bottom lip literally puffing out.

"I have to go," she said. "My two o'clock is messaging me."

"All right, babe," Grayson said. I wondered how much of that was an actual term of endearment and how much of it was because he was shaky on the specifics of which one of his conquests this woman was.

She dove in for a sloppy kiss before heading toward the door. He gave her a sharp pat on her rear, making her squeal as she walked away. I did my best not to roll my eyes.

"Somebody special?" I asked.

Grayson looked over toward the door like he had already forgotten the woman who just walked away from him.

"Yeah, she's a good kid. Always reliable."

I didn't ask any more questions that might inspire him to go into more detail about what he meant by that.

"Coffee?"

"Sure. What do you have new today? Something chocolatey sounds good."

Those were two different things, but I let it go. Without even bothering to describe any of the flavors, I made him a drink that essentially amounted to a chocolate and caramel milkshake with some coffee thrown in for good measure. I set it in front of him.

"Want anything to eat?" I asked. I'd put the drink into a to-go cup just in case he was going to take it on the run, but he settled into a seat at the counter.

"Yeah. One of those biscuit things with the eggs would be good."

I brought the sandwich over to him and went over to help a few customers who had come in. When I went back, Grayson let out a sigh.

"Something bothering you?" I asked.

"Yeah, you know that girl who just moved into the building? The one I was telling you about and who was in here the other day talking to you?" he asked.

"Alex?" I asked.

"Yeah. That's her. I caught up with her when she left here and tried to spend some time with her, and she rejected me. Just straight-out rejected me. Wouldn't let me up to her apartment with her and gave me some lame excuse about needing to wash her hair," Grayson said.

"Well, it doesn't look like you are hurting for attention," I said.

"That's not the point." He pointed to his chest and assumed an expression I figured was meant to be modest. "Look, I don't want to brag or anything, but I get what I want. I'm not used to getting turned down. If there's a situation where someone is getting turned down, and I'm involved, it's me doing the rejecting. But she didn't even think about it. She just shut me down."

"So I guess that's your answer," I said. "Now you can turn your attention to someone else."

"No. That's the thing. I can't stop thinking about her. There's something about that chick. I'm not going to give up that easy," he said, shaking his head.

That wasn't what I wanted to hear. I had to agree, to myself because there was no way I was getting into any kind of personal conversation with Grayson, that there was definitely something about Alex. But that was exactly why I was hoping he would back off. She was clearly able to hold her own with him, but I was hoping he didn't bother her too much.

Grayson stayed a while longer and was leaving just as Barry knocked on the glass at the front of the shop. He was wearing a vibrantly patterned Hawaiian shirt and carrying a tiny puppy who appeared to be wearing a matching miniature version of the same shirt. I went to the door, and he brought the puppy over.

"Nick, meet Banana Split. Banana Split, this is Nick. He's the one who made the cookies for you. Tell him thank you and how much you liked them," Barry said.

With perfect timing, the little dog reached out a paw and placed it on my hand, then wiggled forward and licked me. I laughed.

"You're welcome," I said. "I'll work on a different flavor for you for next time."

Standing there chatting with Barry and the puppy was making me start to question my steadfast position against having a coffee shop dog. Maybe I could figure out a way to work around health codes. I went back into the shop playing around with ideas for new treats I could make for him. I already knew next up was going to be a banana muffin with carob chips and dried cherries.

As I was locking up that evening, Alex got home. The parking spot reserved for her apartment was across the street, so I was able to see her pull in and climb out of the car.

"Hi," she said. "Ready to go home for the night?"

"I've got a quick stop to make first, then yes. How was work?" I asked.

She let out a breath. "I got there by the skin of my teeth, but no one seemed to notice. Thank you again for breakfast. It was great."

I grinned at her. "I'm happy to be your run-thru any time you need it."

Alex smiled at me and waved as she backed toward the door to the building.

"Good night."

I waved. "Good night, Alex."

I watched her until she was in the building, then headed for the shelter to drop off the donations for the day.

Chapter Nine

Alexis

Most people have probably woken up with the first thought on their mind being how much they are looking forward to their first cup of coffee. I certainly was one of them. Many times, it was that promise of a cup of coffee that was the only thing that dug me out from the depths of my blankets, especially on chilly mornings.

That particular morning wasn't chilly, but I was definitely looking forward to going down to the lobby and getting a cup of coffee. In the greater scheme of things, Nick was still a stranger to me. We had only had a couple of conversations, and to be honest, the majority of our communication had occurred in times of chaos and stress. Or vaguely concealed lies about my culinary prowess. But even from those few interactions, I knew he was also really great, and I wanted to get to know him better.

That alone was a somewhat strange feeling to have. It had been a long time since I cared about getting to know anybody, much less a man. It wasn't that I was antisocial or against having any kind of connections in my life. I was just busy and prioritizing the time and energy I had. Though, yes, as much as I didn't want to acknowledge it, I did have the tendency to avoid any type of potential dating relationship with everything in me.

My last serious relationship, truly the only serious relationship I had ever had, hadn't been good for me. And the nasty ending had left me miserable, angry, and feeling pretty much done with the entire concept of sharing my life with anyone. I felt like I'd lost sight of how much my career meant to me and my determination to make something meaningful out of myself and my own life. During that time, I put so much into that man, so much into what he expected of our relationship, and what everyone else expected of our relationship, I'd stopped thinking about myself and the life I wanted.

I wasn't willing to do that again. I didn't want to feel like I was having to choose. I didn't want to choose between a relationship and furthering my career. And I didn't want to choose between a relationship and my friendships that meant so much to me. Gabriela and Valerie had been there for me since I was young and had seen me through my worst. I never wanted anything to come between us.

But for the first time in a very long time, I felt excitement at meeting someone new. I felt a glimmer of something deep inside me, something like optimism, maybe curiosity. I didn't want to go so far as to say hope, but it was a good feeling, and even with the hesitation that was still in the back of my mind, I wanted to give myself that chance to find out what could be there.

I wasn't going to indulge my friends by throwing myself at him. They were very good at picking guys out who they thought would keep me entertained for a while. Both of them said it was just because they wanted me to be happy, but I wasn't sure they really understood what would make me happy. Or maybe they'd just be deep in the trenches of fully committed relationships for so long they'd lost all touch with what the beginning of one looked like and thought they would encourage me to take a dartboard approach to it. Fling myself and if I stuck, great. If not, pick myself back up and fling again.

Flinging wasn't really appealing to me, but Nick seemed like a genuinely good guy. If nothing else, he could be a good friend to have around, especially since I hadn't yet been able to make connections with any of my neighbors. As a matter of fact, I hadn't even seen any of them in person. I was starting to wonder if all the hype about apartments coming available being an extraordinarily rare occurrence was nothing but a sales tactic and the reality was I was living on the entire floor of the building by myself.

I got ready for work faster than usual and headed down early so I'd have more than the thirty seconds I had the other morning when I stopped in and the young guy behind the counter helped me. When I went inside, Nick was behind the counter with a young woman, and I was happy when he glanced over and made eye contact with me. He gestured for me to meet him around the side of the counter.

I felt extremely visible as I wove my way through the crowd that had already accumulated and squeezed up to the small space at the counter.

"Good morning," he said.

"Good morning."

"Would you like your usual?"

"I have a usual?" I asked. He winked at me, and I felt my heart flutter again. I leaned in closer and lowered my voice to a whisper. "Am I allowed to do this? I feel like I'm breaking the rules."

"It's okay," he whispered back. "I know the owner."

I giggled and nodded. "All right. Then I will have my usual."

Nick walked away and came back a few moments later with the same kind of coffee I'd been drinking and a plate with a pastry on it. I glanced at it and then back at him.

"Lemon," he said.

I didn't know if it was a coincidence or if he'd specifically chosen to make those because of the lemon bar incident, but either way, it made me flush a little. I was about to start a conversation with him when I heard someone say my name from behind me. The voice sounded vaguely familiar, but I couldn't place it. I turned around and immediately saw Trevor, the son of one of my father's business associates and one of the guys my family saw as right for me. And who also happened to be horribly obnoxious and beyond not my type.

"Oh, dear lord."

I whipped back around in a vain attempt to shield my face and pretend like I wasn't me and he hadn't actually just looked directly at me. But it didn't do any good. Trevor pushed his way through the crowd, not caring where the line was or who he might be shoving out of the way. As soon as he got near me, he gathered me up into a tight bear hug like we were super close. It felt like his arms were crushing me, and I could feel everyone in the shop staring at us.

I was not enjoying the whole experience. It wasn't horrible, like I was being attacked or anything. It was just intense aggravation. It was annoyance and discomfort in that kind of way of knowing someone your whole life and not especially liking them but having to associate with them because your families are connected and you really don't have much of a choice but to be in their general sphere of existence.

"It's so good to see you, sweetheart," he said, finally releasing me. "I've been missing you so much. I wanted to come surprise you. I've been away for so long, and you were the first person I was thinking about when I got back into town. I couldn't wait to come see you and check out your new place."

Out of the corner of my eye, I saw Nick's expression turn to something close to disappointment. He looked over to the side where there were customers trying to get his attention and walked away to help them. The aggravation turned to frustration and was getting dangerously close to anger as I grabbed Trevor by his arm and tugged him back through the crowd and out the door onto the sidewalk. I didn't even want him in the lobby of the building, much less anywhere near my apartment.

"What the hell are you doing?" I asked.

"I told you. I've missed you while I was away and I wanted to come see you," Trevor said. He stepped up closer to me, reaching for my hips. "Don't I get more of a greeting than that?"

I'd always known Trevor had a crush on me and had been expecting that my father would pressure me into dating him eventually. In his mind, that would mean it was only a matter of time until we got married. It seemed like a perfectly logical arrangement to him. It was beyond out of line for me.

"How did you even know where I moved to?" I demanded.

"Your mother gave me your new address when I came home from traveling abroad," he said. "I went to their house to say hello, and she told me you'd moved."

I should have known.

"Look, Trevor, I'm busy. I've got to get to work," I said. "Welcome back to the States."

I wanted to go back inside and finish my coffee and pastry, but I had a feeling if I did, he would just follow right after me, and I didn't feel like dealing with it. Instead, I headed for my car.

"We should really get together some time. Catch up," Trevor called after me.

I didn't even bother to wave as I climbed into my car and drove away.

Chapter Ten

Nick

Well, that answered that. Alex had a boyfriend. Or at least someone she'd been dating. The guy was clearly into her and had enough of a connection with her to tell her how much he'd missed her since he'd been gone. That wasn't something a casual acquaintance would say.

But of course, she did. I should have expected that. Alex was gorgeous, friendly, and obviously successful. It would only make sense for her to have a boyfriend. I felt ridiculous for thinking she was flirting with me. I was so wrapped up in my own puppy dog-eyes crush on her that I'd convinced myself that her friendliness was something more.

I decided I wasn't going to let it get to me too much. After all, there really wasn't anything I could do about it. And it wasn't like I had a ton of time or energy invested in her or any type of actual relationship with her beyond the very beginnings of friendship we'd started laying down. I'd been enjoying seeing her, and I liked talking to her, but I couldn't let myself get too worked up over realizing something that should have been so clear to me. If I found her as fantastic as I did, obviously other people would, too.

I indulged myself for a few minutes wondering where this guy was when she was moving in and why he hadn't been there to help her, but then it occurred to me he had said he was away and that probably meant he had just gotten back into town. He wouldn't be that excited to see her and then wait several days.

It might have also explained why she seemed as frazzled as she did when she was moving in. I could imagine most people would be frustrated and stressed if they were moving, and their significant other wasn't even there to help them.

She hadn't had the luxury of delaying moving into her new apartment; she'd had to take the day that the owners of the building told her it was available or risk them choosing to move on to someone else, and it struck me that it didn't seem like his appearance was planned. She hadn't been expecting to see him, and he'd said he was there to surprise her. She wouldn't have been able to plan around him coming back, anyway.

Fortunately, I didn't have too much downtime to let my brain wander around finding all the ways this could bother me. The shop got even busier, and I was able to throw myself into filling orders. Close to lunchtime, a friendly voice brought a smile to my face.

"Hey there, stranger."

I looked up and saw Penelope, an old friend who drifted around in life like an autumn leaf. It was hard to predict exactly where she was going or what she was going to be doing next, but whatever it was, she was going to be vibrant and impressive while she did it.

"Hey," I said, coming around the side of the counter to gather her up in a hug. "It's been forever."

"I know," she said, fluttering her hands beside her head. "Everything has just been so crazy."

"What's been going on with you?" I asked.

One of the multitude of rings on one hand got caught in some of the tight, bouncy curls that expanded from the sides of her head and came to her shoulders. She didn't even miss a beat as she untangled it.

"Well, you know I was writing that book," she said.

I gave her a questioning look as I went around the counter again to start making what I remembered to be her favorite coffee. The darkest, strongest brew I had with two espresso shots, almond milk, hazelnut syrup, and enough sugar to fuel an entire kindergarten.

"Book?" I asked. "I thought you were working on the paintings for the art installation at the museum."

"I was," she said. "But I got so inspired by the work I was doing with the paintings that I realized there was a story inside me that was just screaming out to be told. Usually, I can tell those stories through painting. It's what I do. Right?"

"Right," I said, agreeing with her even though trying to define Penelope just by being a painter was an almost comical simplification.

She had always dabbled in enough things to make it seem like she was simultaneously living several lives. One thing she said to me when we first met back in college was that we only get a very limited time here on this earth, and most people think they get to choose just one path to follow and one life they are going to lead for the entire time they are here. But she refused to do that. She was going to do as much as she possibly could, be as many things as she possibly could, and live as many lives as she possibly could in the time she had allotted. After all, how could she know for sure she'd chosen the right one if she was only going to do one?

"Well, as I was listening to this story being told within me and trying to figure out how I was going to put it out on the canvas, I realized it just wasn't going to work. Painting simply wasn't the medium to tell the story. That, of course, wasn't commentary on the story or on the art, but on me as an artist. I needed to be able to adapt myself to the whims of the story and tell it the way it wanted to be told," she said.

"Which was written," I said.

I grabbed a few treats out of the display case and brought them along with the coffee over to a table in the far corner of the shop. It was a rare time when both of my employees were there during an overlapped shift, which meant I wasn't even actually supposed to be there. I could take a few minutes to talk to an old friend and attempt to figure out what it was she was telling me.

"Exactly," Penelope said as we sat down and she reached to break a chunk off a pistachio blondie. "Which is strange because writing has never been my strong suit. It feels so dry and distant. Painting or sculpting or glassblowing or interpretive dance are much more alive. People enjoying the pieces can feel them. But this story needed to be told with the written word, and so I devoted myself to learning this skill."

I felt like we were getting further and further away from the starting point of the story where she was going to tell me what she'd been up to since I'd last seen her a few months back, but there was really no way for me to stop it. Penelope wasn't one you could get back on track easily. Any attempt to redirect the conversation would inevitably end up as a detour that just ended up meandering even further.

As she talked, I made eye contact with Kristie and gestured for a coffee. Usually, I wouldn't ask either of them to wait on me, but I couldn't find a good space in the flow of the conversation to tell Penelope I would be right back. There was also the chance that if I got up and went to get coffee, something would strike her fancy, and she'd wander away. I'd rather get the rest of the story before that happened.

I drank my coffee as I listened to her tell me how she'd gone from being inspired by her painting to write a book and then for that book to inspire her to become a migrant farm worker for the harvest season, which then segued into a stint with a traveling carnival where she met a woman who eventually taught her to quilt. It all had a very mouse and cookie vibe to it.

"Living with them at the commune for the last two months was incredible. But I really felt as if I'd achieved all I could in that sphere, at least for this particular time in my life, and so I came back to finish the work on my installation," she said.

It was so much to take in, I needed a few seconds to let it all settle before I could respond. Part of me thought about how well she and Barry might get along. But another part of me feared for the future of humanity as I knew it if they were to combine forces.

"How about you?" she asked. "This place looks like it just keeps getting more popular."

I looked around at the customers and nodded.

"Business has been really good," I said. "It's great with all the people who live in the building, but a lot of my regulars actually don't even live here."

"Are you still getting offers to buy it?" she asked.

"Yeah. A guy was just in here the other day, as a matter of fact. They've started talking about franchising and having several of the shops around the city, packaged food, consistent menus. All the things I wanted to avoid completely when I was planning The Coffee Shop. The whole point of it is to not be another corporate spot where you can eat the exact same thing in all fifty thousand locations and feel like you don't even know where you are when you go into one," I said.

"And that's what makes this place as great as it is. How about that TV guy? Did you hear from him again?" she asked.

Penelope was the only person I'd told about the TV executive reaching out to me from a culinary network about a reality show they wanted to cast me on. She'd come in the day I heard from him, and I talked it out with her, deciding almost instantly against doing it.

"He's emailed a few more times. He still seems really interested, but I just don't think it's something I want to do. I don't want to be on camera or turning this into a competition."

"You do what is right for you and screw everyone else," she said matter-of-factly. "In the end, you're the only one you really have to answer to."

That night when I got home, I noticed I had a couple of missed calls and voicemails. I tended to ignore my phone during work. There were few things in this world more annoying to me than seeing people standing around with their phones constantly in their hands, as if they weren't capable of functioning if they couldn't scroll through social media or news. I couldn't imagine not being able to just exist in the world for ten seconds without being entertained by a little box.

I was especially aggravated when I went into a place of business and saw employees messing with their phones. It made me feel like they were wasting time and not really putting care and energy into the work they were supposed to be doing. So I made it a point not to look at my phone unless I was on break and thought I might get an important call. That day I hadn't even looked.

When I checked what I missed, I let out a sigh. They were all from my ex.

Holly and I had been together for a few years, and there was definitely a time when I'd thought she might be The One. But looking back, I could see how things weren't great between us toward the end of the relationship. There was already some tension, and things weren't feeling the way they used to, then I got my inheritance from my mother.

Immediately, Holly started making plans for the money. She wanted to use it to travel around and have a more exciting life. I was focused on establishing my business and getting a strong foundation in life. Her bitterness and resentment toward the fact that I pointed out the money was mine and I would decide how to use it, and it wasn't going to be blown on travel and shopping, led to our breakup.

It was very difficult at first, but I got over it. I thought it was all behind me, but the messages I heard as I played them back just told me it wasn't. Apparently, she'd gotten it into her mind that she was entitled to a cut of the profits of my business. In message after message after message, she outlined how she deserved a large percentage of the money my business made now and into the future. She even demanded I give her an executive position within the company, which I clearly didn't even have.

We were "basically married," she proclaimed, and that meant she had a very serious interest in the company and deserved to benefit from its success. That she was my "support system" and offered unconditional love and encouragement while helping me come up with all the ideas, the menu, and even the name.

All of it was a lie, but that didn't really matter. I knew she could cause me some trouble with all this nonsense. I was going to have to figure out how to shut her down quickly without people knowing about it.

Feeling aggravated, I took a shower and went to bed.

Chapter Eleven

Alexis

The next morning was the beginning of one of those days when I knew I was going to need plenty of coffee. Not that there were really mornings of my life when I didn't need coffee, but this one stood out as being particularly pressing in the coffee area. I had a whole evening of maid of honor duties planned for after work, and I wasn't particularly looking forward to it. I already knew it was going to be a stressful, busy day at the office, and it was going to take all my energy and attempts at a sunny disposition to get me through everything.

Hence the need for coffee. And lots of it.

I'd found my own coffeemaker and set it up in my kitchen, which is how I had a massive ugly travel cup full of a very basic coffee with me already as I made my way through the lobby. But I needed the good stuff. The travel cup was just a backup plan to keep me pumped up as needed throughout the rest of the day. The coffee I was planning on ordering from Nick was going to jolt my day to a start and act as a preemptive self-reward for getting through everything.

The coffee shop was surprisingly quiet as I walked through the door. There were only a few customers sitting at the counter or at tables, and the line was short. I was going to go ahead and take that as a good omen. Even if it actually meant nothing but that I had managed to time my visit effectively, I was going to take anything I could get that day.

I smiled as I stepped up to the counter to make my order. I was all prepared with a cute comment about getting special treatment from the owner when Alex glanced over at me. There wasn't as much of his usual brightness when he flashed a fast smile. I stood waiting while he finished a conversation with a man sitting at the counter and then came over to me.

"Good morning," he said. "How are you today?"

It was perfectly pleasant and friendly, but far less bubbly and welcoming than I was accustomed to from him. I looked at him for a second, wondering what was going on and waiting for him to give me some sort of explanation, but he just looked back.

"Good morning."

"Can I get you something? Coffee?" Nick asked.

It seemed ridiculous to admit it even to myself, but that stung a little. There was absolutely no reason why it should have. He owned a coffee shop. I was visiting said coffee shop. It made perfect sense that he would inquire about what I might want to order. Even though he had taken it upon himself to bring me the same type of coffee nearly every time I saw him. Usually with a special treat or snack of some kind.

But that wasn't the norm. He didn't do that for every customer, so I really shouldn't have expected it all the time from him. After all, he'd said he wanted to welcome me to the building. Maybe now that I'd been here for several days, he felt like he had finished his responsibilities as unofficial building welcoming committee and had transitioned into just a regular customer level of interaction.

It bothered me to think that way. It made me feel like I had done something wrong, or at the very least that I had misinterpreted how he was feeling about me. Neither one of them felt very good. I couldn't imagine what I might have done to upset him or make him not want to be as warm toward me. But it embarrassed me, and disappointed me if I was going to be completely honest, to think that the little flutters of feelings I was getting were one-sided.

But there was nothing I could do about it. The window of throwing myself at him, if there ever really was a window of time where that would have been appropriate, had long-since passed. And I really didn't have the time or energy to devote too much into understanding it and trying to change it. At least he was still there to make sure I had the coffee I needed.

"That ham and cheese croissant sounds really good," I said, noticing it on the menu. "I'll take one of those for breakfast. And if you've made the roasted vegetable panini, I'll have that for lunch later."

"Just one or will your boyfriend be joining you for lunch?" Nick asked.

It was such a strange, out of left field question it took me a couple of beats to even figure out what it was he was saying.

"My boyfriend?" I asked.

"Yeah. The guy who was here the other day. He seemed really excited to come here to surprise you. He must have been gone a long time. I couldn't really see your face, but he looked really happy," he said.

I rolled my eyes in aggravation so hard I thought I might topple over.

"You're talking about that guy who came in here the other day when I was ordering coffee?" I said. "The one I dragged outside with me and then didn't end up coming back?" He nodded, and I shook my head, letting out a relieved smile because at least now I understood what was going on in his mind. "That wasn't my boyfriend."

"He wasn't?" Nick asked.

"Not at all. Full disclosure, he definitely wants to be my boyfriend, but he's not going to be. Ever. That would be Trevor. He is the son of one of my father's business associates. My father and his father both think we'd be the perfect couple and should have married by now, so they find all kinds of creative ways to push us together with the belief that eventually we'll end up the perfect husband and wife to continue on with our family ways," I said.

"Your families believe in arranged marriages?" he asked, sounding slightly bewildered.

I laughed and shook my head. "Not exactly. It's more just that my family and the kinds of people my parents like to associate with have clear ideas of what they think their children should have in a partner, and they come to little agreements about pairing them up. Nothing formal. We don't have betrothal ceremonies or have fairies come and bestow wishes on us as newborns or anything. But it's not unusual for couples to kind of be guided together for years until it just becomes inevitable."

I explained a little more about the way my family looked at me and what they thought my life should be versus what I wanted my life to be. Nick looked relieved, and I realized I liked that he felt that way. It meant maybe I wasn't so far off the mark with how I thought he felt about me.

"Is that the way things were for your friend I met? Gabriela?" he asked.

"No. She and Dean didn't need any encouragement when it came to finding each other. Their families started asking when they were getting engaged a few months after they officially started dating, but they took their time so Dean could get his career really established. Now it's all about the wedding. I'm actually going over to her place after work today to do some wedding preparations, and then her bachelorette party is this weekend," I said.

Nick looked at me with a slightly cocked eyebrow. "You don't sound particularly excited about that."

"Can you keep a secret?" I asked.

He leaned a little closer and nodded. "Sure."

"I hate weddings. Especially ones I have to be in," I whispered.

He grinned. "The scandal."

I left the shop feeling happy. I really enjoyed the friendship we were building, and it was nice that I was starting to feel like this building really was home.

It was a mercifully smoother day at work than I had been anticipating, so I had more energy and space in my brain left than I expected to as I headed over to Gabriela's apartment. I definitely felt like I needed that. I wasn't looking forward to the hours of handling wedding details that were ahead of me. I adored Gabriela. She was my best friend, and I would do absolutely anything for her, as evidenced by me agreeing to be her maid of honor and throwing myself fully into the role without hesitation or outward complaint. I would never make her sad or uncomfortable about anything to do with her wedding.

But what I'd confided in Nick was true. I knew in the eyes of everyone around me, including my dearest friends, I was supposed to be full of excitement when it came to any wedding. I was supposed to love all the festivities and the pomp and circumstance and think it was so beautiful and romantic. I had friends who fell all over themselves at every single wedding they went to, and that could easily be ten or more each year depending on their friend circles and their parents' business associations.

I just couldn't get into it that much. I didn't like all the drama and theatrics that went into a wedding. It all seemed like far too much froth and over-the-top obsessing over meaningless details designed more or less to impress people. Big weddings always struck me as being more about the performance and the party than the marriage, when that was really what should matter.

I would never say that to Gabriela, though. Just like I didn't say it to Valerie three years ago when it was her turn. These were their days, and they should have them exactly how they wanted them, so I did everything they wanted and needed of me. And then ate two extra pieces of wedding cake and talked to the bartender throughout the night so I could at least enjoy myself and avoid the wedding reception game of getting set up for dances and drinks. These parties could end up feeling like thinly veiled speed dating, and I did my best to steer clear of it.

The main focus of that evening's gathering with Gabriela and the rest of her bridesmaids was to fill welcome bags for the out-of-town guests and write thank you notes for the gifts the bride had received at her shower a couple of weeks before. We had several tables set up with all the items she had chosen for the bags, and each of us were filling bags and setting them aside on another table so we could later add tags with the guests' names.

I added a pair of slippers and a tube of locally made lip balm to the bag I was holding and moved over to the artisan toiletry items we'd picked up. I couldn't help but smile as I put in the soap, little bottle of lotion, face cloth, and handmade cotton loofah that Gabriela and had I found at the gift boutique where I bought the lemon bars. I hadn't told her that story yet. It was funny, and I knew she would laugh about it, but I felt protective of it. Like it was something Nick and I shared. Our own little private joke.

Gabriela looked slightly flushed and was grinning the entire time we filled the bags and she wrote notes. It was obvious how excited she was getting with the wedding coming so close. When we weren't talking about the ceremony and her honeymoon plans, we were gushing over Valerie and how soon the baby was coming. One thing I did have to commend Gabriela for was that as much as she joked about worrying Valerie would have her baby at the wedding, she hadn't shown any actual signs of being jealous or thinking Valerie was taking attention from her. She had her visions for her day, but she wasn't a bridezilla. That made the process far more enjoyable than it could have been.

I loved seeing how happy she was, even if it did give me a little twinge in my heart. I'd made the choice to be single, but there were times when it definitely didn't feel like a choice, and I wondered what it would be like to be so in love and so happy.

Chapter Twelve

Nick

That Friday night, I couldn't sleep. Bouts of insomnia or something I had dealt with occasionally since I was a teenager, and that week I had the extra weight on my mind of Holly and her complete nonsense. I still hadn't decided exactly what I was going to do about her demands.

There was no way I would ever stay if she had anything to do with the development of The Coffee Shop or with its success. The closest thing she did to supporting me through building the business or contributing to creating it was that we were in a relationship when I first started talking about opening a coffee shop, and she listened to me while I bandied around ideas for the name of the shop, items I might have on the menu, and the way I might decorate the space.

That was the extent of how much she was involved. Holly had been so bitter about me not wanting to put all of my inheritance into lavish vacations and expensive shopping sprees that she made it very clear how she felt about the shop and my devotion to it every time I started talking about it. Which meant we ended up talking less and less in the last part of our relationship. Looking back at that time, I knew I'd become completely wrapped up in getting the shop off the ground.

Some people might say I had neglected her and our relationship in favor of the shop. But there wasn't a single part of me that regretted that decision. Having the shop was a huge dream of mine. It was the greatest accomplishment of my life, and I was going to do it right. I didn't want to be another one of those flash-in-the-pan businesses that got off to a great start and fizzled almost immediately.

I figured if she really was supposed to be my partner, she would be genuinely supportive of me and want to be right there by my side helping me. I didn't push her away because I didn't want her involved or because I wanted to do everything on my own. If she had been excited for me or wanted to help me, I would have welcomed it. That would have shown me our relationship really was important.

Instead, she showed the kind of person she really was, and she let the money and the shop become a massive sore point for her. What started as her listening to me talk about everything with detached disinterest turned into stony silence and then eventually anger and outbursts every time I mentioned it. She would say I was doing it on purpose, that I was only going through the process because I knew it bothered her and that I was trying to hurt her. That if I really loved her, I would see how much this whole pursuit was bothering her and would drop it.

And there was a time when I thought maybe she was right. I felt guilty about our relationship falling apart and thought maybe it was my fault. But fortunately, I talked myself out of that fairly quickly. Maybe I did bury myself in getting ready to open and didn't have much time for anything else in my life, but opening my shop was the biggest and most important thing I had ever done. If our relationship was solid and meant to be a life partnership, it wouldn't have created a wedge; it would have bonded us more closely.

Instead, the relationship fractured, and Holly left before I'd even opened. Now all of a sudden, she was back and rewriting history to favor herself. I hadn't been following her life and really didn't know anything that was going on with her at the time but knew through my siblings keeping me filled in about the new of the old neighborhood that several of our former shared friend group had gone through divorces in the last year.

My sister had nearly burst before being able to spill the gossip about each of the couples, including Paul and Divinity Morris, who everybody thought was the golden couple that could never be apart. Only, Divinity had run off with the mail carrier after her homebased multilevel marketing business started requiring a tremendous number of deliveries to show up at the house.

Or Cristel and Mark Woolman, who seemed like the type who were really going to get to big places together. Cristel had worked hard for years, sometimes at two or three jobs, to support Mark through school so he could start his career as a lawyer. As soon as he made partner, Cristel found out he was cheating on her, and she was booted right out the door without a single cent to her name. The last I heard they were still embroiled in a legal battle over her request for alimony and his assertion he shouldn't need to support her since she'd clearly proven she was more than capable of supporting herself.

I couldn't help but wonder if it was those stories, and the other similar ones that had played out among the doomed couples, that had sparked inspiration in Holly's mind. Maybe she saw her friends not getting what they deserved and thought she was wronged in her mind, so she should be compensated, just without the benefit of the marriage or the divorce to go along with it.

Though I had absolutely no doubt in my mind that what she was saying about her involvement was wrong, I knew she was capable of creating many problems for me in this situation. She could drag me into court. She could go public with her assertions and damage my reputation. She could do any number of things that would cause me a tremendous amount of trouble. I wasn't sure what the best way to handle it would be. How I could be proactive and take care of the situation before it had a chance to turn into anything.

Going over all the different scenarios and options in my head was keeping me awake, and in the early hours of Saturday morning, I decided it was useless to keep lying in bed staring at the ceiling. If I wasn't going to be able to sleep, I might as well make use of the time. I got up, got dressed, and headed into the shop so I could get some extra baking done. Hopefully it would use up my excess energy and help clear my thoughts.

I had a few custom orders for picnics for the next day, so I started off by getting a few items for those underway. I got the baskets lined up and pieces of cloth inside, then added a few little basic items I'd sourced from local businesses like jars of local honey, ground mustard, and pieces of a couple of different kinds of cheese from a cheese maker I had befriended while sourcing product for my menu.

When I had trays of breadsticks and cheese straws baking in the oven alongside loaves of bread and shells for fruit tarts, I turned my attention to an idea that had been bouncing around in my head since talking to Alex earlier in the week.

I knew that was the night she was at the bachelorette party with her friends, and she had mentioned that they were planning on coming back to Alex's apartment to spend the night. I thought it would be cute to make some miniature wedding cakes for the next day to give them to help battle the hangovers I figured they'd be dealing with. I'd even gotten several airplane bottles of liquor I thought I'd include with cups of coffee in a little care basket, some "hair of the dog" to help get them over the hump.

As I was working on the cakes, I heard a strange noise out in the front of the shop. Coming out of the kitchen, I saw Alex standing on the outside, pounding on the glass. I'd kept the lights off so as to not call attention to me being there, but she must have either noticed the light from the kitchen or caught sight of me since the kitchen was partially open to the rest of the shop.

Alex was pounding her hands against the window, shouting my name through the glass. I knew the security guard was going to come soon, and there was no need for that. I didn't want her to get into any trouble or be embarrassed, and we definitely didn't need to attract the attention of any of the other people living in the building. I rushed to the door to open it, and Alex tumbled in on me. I caught her and helped right her back on her feet.

Gabriela was behind her, along with a heavily pregnant woman and two others I didn't recognize. They were all dressed for the bachelorette party in matching glittery dresses, towering high heels, and some questionable accessories. Gabriela was perhaps the most tasteful of the group with her pink sash proclaiming her the bride-to-be and a sparkly tiara perched on her head. The other girls were wearing flashing glow lights around their wrists and necks, necklaces with shot glasses attached, and headbands with what appeared to be small bobbing penises at the end. It was all quite the visual.

The only one of them who didn't appear at least on the tipsy side was the pregnant one, who watched the rest of them looking exhausted and a touch bewildered by the whole experience. At least, I thought the expression was bewildered. It was a little difficult to tell coming from behind large plastic eyeglasses with lights flashing around the rims.

"Hi," Alex said when she was almost stable on her feet again. "Hi, Nick."

I smiled. "Hi, Alex. Are you doing okay?"

"Fine. Just fine. We were out partying. Oh, hey, you don't know everybody." She looked at the other girls and gestured at me. "Hey, this is Nick." She said my name as a short sound with a strong, clicking emphasis on the 'k' at the end. "Isn't he cute? I think he's cute. Anyway, Nick makes coffee." She looked at me again. "We were at the bachelorette party and now we want food."

She hadn't actually gotten around to introducing me to the other girls, but that was fine. I figured the chances of her remembering this come morning were slim to none. Including her calling me cute. Not that I was going to let it slide. She needed to hear all about this.

"Come on in," I said. "I'll get some coffee going for you."

The pregnant woman headed directly for the couch and dropped down onto it with a groan. I couldn't imagine that being a part of a rowdy bachelorette party at that stage of pregnancy was easy for her. Or particularly fun. But she was there, bobbing penises, flashing lights, and all, to support her friend. She closed her eyes, and I was pretty sure she was fast asleep within a second and a half, but she'd fought a good fight.

I went behind the counter and got the coffeemaker going. I didn't want to give them anything too strong. What they really needed right about then was a good night of sleep, so I didn't want to pump them full of too much caffeine and keep them awake. I smiled as I filled a few plates with snacks and treats for them, listening to them chatter behind me. I liked that Alex thought of me.

Chapter Thirteen

Alexis

The smell of the coffee brewing was glorious. It beat the hell out of the smoky, alcohol-soaked bars we had been hanging out in all night. And I wasn't even going to start on the strip club. That had been Tracy's contribution to the plans for the night. It sounded like fun in theory. In practice, not so much.

The best decision that was made for the entire night was hiring a limo to drive us around to the different party stops. The company I chose was highly experienced at providing transportation for bachelorette parties and had come highly recommended. As soon as they arrived to pick us up, I could tell why.

The limo was bubblegum pink with matching running lights and large, clear crystals embedded around the windows and license plate. Inside, the driver had equipped the car with our first round of drinks for the night, chocolates, and some props and games. Music blaring, we took off into town, and there was no turning back.

I walked up to the counter and leaned against it to hold myself upright.

"Can I help you?" I asked, then started giggling, my forehead dropping to my hands on the top of the counter. "Did you hear that? I asked if I could help you. At your counter. That's what you usually ask people."

Nick chuckled as he continued brewing coffee and putting together little sandwiches.

"I heard that," he said. "But I'm fine. Go on and sit down with your friends. I'll bring all this over to you in just a minute."

"Are you sure?" I asked. The world swayed a little bit, and I caught myself, gripping the counter harder to stop from tipping over.

Nick watched me for a silent second like he was waiting to make sure I'd gotten through that, then nodded.

"I'm sure. Go relax. I'll be over there in a second."

I went back over to the chairs where the other girls were sitting and plopped down into one of them, still watching Nick behind the counter. He was so cute. Like really cute. Did I say that out loud in front of him? Did he hear me say that?

It didn't matter. I was drunk. He wasn't going to remember.

Valerie was already asleep, but the rest of us were wide awake and still riding the waves of the party when Nick came over carrying a tray with large cups of coffee for all of us and a carafe to set in the middle of the table. He went back and returned a second later with two big serving trays full of sandwiches, crackers and cheese, tarts, cookies, and muffins.

"No lemon bars?" I asked, then dissolved into laughter.

Nick let out a short laugh and shook his head. "No. No lemon bars this time."

Gabriela narrowed her eyes at me. "Why is that so funny?"

"Because he made them," I said, pointing at Nick.

She looked at him, then burst out laughing. Nick shook his head, laughing under his breath.

"It looks like you ladies had a good time tonight," he said. "Gabriela, congratulations on your upcoming wedding, by the way."

Gabriela threw her arm up in the air while holding her coffee the way she had with many a cocktail throughout the evening. This time it was a bit more treacherous, with hot coffee sloshing over the side and coming down toward her. She managed to avoid it hitting her, but it splashed on the table and the floor. Nick didn't seem to mind.

"Wooo," Gabriela shouted. "Bride!" She then settled down and became suddenly serious. "Thank you. I'm really looking forward to it."

"Tell me about the party," he said. "I've obviously never been to a bachelorette party."

Tracy gasped. "You haven't? Oh my gosh, you should. They are so fun."

I giggled, and Nick made eye contact with me and smiled.

"Did you have fun?" he asked.

"Yes, I did," I said. "Most of the time. I mean, the stripper was a little on the iffy side. I don't think his uniform would have protected him from a fire one bit. There was far too much just hanging out that would have been a very serious burn hazard. And another one just kept doing the same move over and over again like he'd forgotten the rest of what he was supposed to do. But there were a lot of women there who were really happy to see those moves, so maybe he knew what he was doing."

"Sounds like it," Nick said.

"But you know what was not fun? Grayson," I said.

Nick's face dropped. "Grayson was there?"

"Not as a stripper," I clarified, wagging my finger. "That is not part of his official duties. It is not one of the many services the Bentley is proud to offer its residents. No, he showed up at one of the bars. I don't know which one." I looked at Gabriela. "Do you know which one?" She shrugged. "We don't know which one. But, anyway, we were just there playing our bridal party bingo and trying to find someone for Gabriela to kiss twenty times to get the corner square, and he showed up."

"I did not want to kiss him," Gabriela said.

"She did not," I confirmed. "But he was all about wanting to be a part of the bachelorette party. He just kept coming over to us and trying to buy us drinks and be involved in the game. There was even a girl there with him, and he just left her standing there by the bar. And she stayed! Can you believe that? She was watching him act like that and she seriously just stayed there at the bar, drinking her drink, looking at him like she was wondering how long it was going to take him to come back.

"So then we left and went to the next bar. And guess what happened? He showed up there, too. Like he followed us or something. But, of course, he acted like it was all a coincidence. Like everybody just casually goes to multiple bars in the same night and happens to have a whole tray of pink Jell-O shots with glitter rims when they run into a group of their not friends."

"Wait, Grayson showed up at the next bar?" Nick asked.

"Yep. He did. With pink Jell-O shots and glitter rims. I don't even know where he got those. They weren't on the menu. And he tried to feed one to me." I shuddered. "He is so rude. And he seriously can't take a hint. I told him this was a bachelorette party. It was for us girls to enjoy some time together and to celebrate the bride-to-be as we get ready for her wedding. And he just wouldn't leave us alone. He kept trying to get us to dance with him or sit on his lap or take body shots with him. He is just way too much."

Nick looked like he was not happy hearing this. "Alex, you need to say something about this to somebody," he said.

"I just did," she said.

"No, I don't mean me. You could report him to the building management. They should know how he's treating women, especially someone who lives in the building," he said.

"I don't know. I don't want to cause trouble," I said.

"Alex, I don't want to overstep my bounds here, and I definitely don't want to make you feel like I'm trying to speak for you or anything, but I also really don't want this to go any further. If you aren't comfortable saying something, I can submit an anonymous complaint to building management just letting them know what I've observed and heard. I don't have to mention your name or tell them what you told me tonight specifically. Would that be all right with you?" he asked.

I stared at him for a few seconds, just to work through all those words. There were so many words.

"Maybe," I finally said.

Nick smiled softly and brushed a piece of my hair away from my face. "Okay. We'll talk about this again some other time. I'll remind you later since you probably won't remember it."

"Why not?" I asked. "Oh. Right. The alcohol. Yeah, that's probably for the best."

"Oh! Tell him about the karaoke!" Tracy suddenly said, making me jump a little.

I was glad to get away from talking about the creepy building tour guide and tell Nick all about the karaoke bar we found while trying to find our next spot. We thought it was just a late-night sushi bar where we could get a snack but quickly found out it was karaoke night and ended up singing much of Gabriela's requested reception playlist.

As we talked, Nick sat close beside me, pressing back against me when I leaned into him and occasionally filling my coffee mug or choosing another treat or snack for me to try. He was so sweet. And cute. I felt like I'd already thought about how cute he was, but he was just really cute. Maybe it was the cocktails talking, which would make sense since I'd had a lot of them so they'd be pretty loud.

Valerie had fallen asleep immediately after we got into the shop, and after a while, I noticed Sarah had also fallen asleep on the table, and Tracy was starting to droop. Gabriela was still conscious, but she was looking very tired.

"Alex, I think it's time for us to go upstairs and get some sleep," she said.

I nodded. "That's probably a good idea." I gave her my key. "Take the girls on up. I'm going to help Nick clean up. I'll be up in a bit."

"I'll help," she offered.

"No," Tracy said emphatically. "I need to go to bed."

Nick laughed. "It's fine. I can handle this. You ladies go on up and get some sleep."

"No, I'm not going to leave you to do it all yourself. I'm going to help you," I insisted.

My friends left, and Nick watched them walk across the lobby to the elevator to make sure they got there safely. I helped him clean up, thanking him for everything. It didn't take long to get everything cleaned up, and when we were finished, he gestured toward the door.

"Do you want me to walk you up to your apartment?" he asked.

I shook my head. "No. That's okay. I can do it. Thank you."

I started toward the door and stumbled, my shoe sliding on the floor so I nearly fell. Nick rushed to catch me, holding me against him for a second so I could get my bearings. I was very aware of the warmth of his body and the strength of his arms holding me. I didn't argue with him wanting to escort me the rest of the way.

He typed my code into the elevator, and we rode up in silence. I stole glances at him out of the corner of my eye. I hadn't asked him why he was at the shop so late. The limo driver informed us we'd reached the end of our time and brought us back to the building, but we were hungry and still a bit loopy from the party. I didn't mention it to any of the other girls, and I didn't even want to admit it to myself, but I'd been thinking about Nick throughout the night, so when Gabriela mentioned she'd like some late-night snacks, he was the first thing that came to mind.

We got to my apartment, and I turned to Nick.

"Thank you again. Good night."

I went to kiss him on the cheek, but my aim was off, and I ended up hitting the side of his lips. We both paused, our mouths hovering near each other for a second before he leaned in for another kiss. It was soft and gentle, like he was testing it. Our lips parted, and we looked into each other's eyes. Nick's hands found my hips and pulled me against him as he ducked his head down for a deeper kiss.

Everything in me lit up with that kiss. I pressed against him, my arms looping around his neck. I didn't want it to end, but when it did, I gestured at the door.

"Do you want to..."

"I'm going to get going," he said. "I'm going to crash in my office for a bit before I have to open up the shop. Good night."

He walked away, and I watched him until he was in the elevator again. A bit miffed at his flat-out rejection, I went inside and flopped down on my bed, not even bothering to change out of my dress.

Chapter Fourteen

Nick

Considering how late it already was, it seemed like a waste of the very short amount of time I had before the shop needed to open to walk home. It was only a few blocks, but that would mean going home, going to sleep, getting back up, and coming all the way back when instead I could just go into my office, the one fully enclosed area of the shop that wasn't the walk-in freezer, and catch a few winks on the couch in there.

I always kept extra clothes in the office just for that type of situation, so I set the alarm on my phone for just a few extra minutes before the time I would usually arrive at the shop and settled in. I expected for my insomnia from earlier to continue, but I ended up drifting off quickly.

When the alarm rudely broke through the very pleasant dream I was having, I opened my eyes to my very first thoughts being of Alex and the kiss from the night before. It was one of those kisses that felt like it had been building up for a long time even though we hadn't known each other for all that long. I knew it didn't start out as an intentional kiss the way it ended up. Alex was saying good night and obviously wanted to kiss me on the cheek, but when her soft lips overlapped my mouth a little, I couldn't resist.

It was a pretty great kiss. I loved the way her body felt wrapped up in my arms, pressed against me so our hearts were beating against each other. I liked the way she tasted, all coffee and sugar and the faint lingering hint of alcohol. It made me wonder what she would taste like if the kiss didn't follow a night of partying. Then the thought went through my head that I wondered if she would even remember the kiss.

I had my strong doubts she was going to come into that day with clear memories of everything that had happened the night before. I wouldn't go so far as to say she was blackout drunk, and I thought the entire night would be wiped as soon as she fell asleep. But she had definitely enjoyed her fair share of shots and mixed drinks, and that made for some fuzziness the next day.

She would likely remember some of the earlier parts of the night, like the limo coming to pick them up and the first bar that they'd visited. She'd probably even remember the next stop. And I was almost positive she would remember Grayson there annoying them. That part really bothered me. I hated that he was so persistent with her, that he wasn't taking her telling him no and not showing him any interest as an actual answer. He definitely had the idea that a woman saying no was just a challenge. It made him want to conquer her even more, and that made my skin crawl.

But would she remember the way she'd flirted with me? The way she'd leaned against me and brushed her thigh against mine while we were sitting at the table and they were telling me stories about their night? Would she remember the way she'd looked into my eyes and licked her lips while we were cleaning up, making me want that kiss by her door more than I could even say?

And would she remember the kiss?

I hoped that she would. But maybe I hoped that she wouldn't. It was a strange situation. It was an awesome kiss, but I had followed it up with summarily rejecting her when she obviously wanted me to come inside her apartment with her. Now I wasn't sure what I was supposed to do next.

I knew I had done the right thing when I was standing there in the hallway, looking at her door and the expression in her eyes, knowing she was about to invite me in. As much as everything in me was telling me how much I wanted to go in with her, Alex was drunk. Very drunk. She'd gotten herself together a bit more throughout the night with the food and the coffee in her, but she was definitely not in any kind of position to be making those decisions.

I never would have felt right about going in with her when she was in that condition. But it certainly put me in a weird position. Did I make a move? Did I go to her apartment and take her in my arms and kiss her when she opened the door? Or when she came in for coffee?

Not even going that far, was I supposed to say something to her the next time she came into the shop? Since I had no idea how much she actually remembered, I would have no way of evaluating how she acted. If she came in and didn't act any special kind of way, didn't try to flirt with me more or kiss me or anything, it could mean that she didn't remember the kiss and had no reason to be acting any differently. Or it could mean she did remember the kiss and was embarrassed or wished it hadn't happened, so she was taking the approach of just pretending it hadn't happened and trying to move forward with as little awkwardness as possible.

That made me wonder if I should remind her of any of it. Should I tell her what happened and ask her out? Or maybe just ask her out without talking about the kiss and wait to see if the chemistry was still there? Mentioning it seemed to run the high risk of embarrassing her and making her feel like I was taunting her, while not mentioning it and still asking her out felt exploitive, like I was taking advantage of the situation.

I had never been in this particular kind of situation, but I hadn't even been in any sort of position with a woman in a long time. It was making me feel like an awkward, gangly kid in high school. This was one of those moments when I felt like I needed to be able to write a note and ask her if she liked me and to check yes or no. Not that it had ever worked out that way for me. And I sincerely doubted it would go over well now. I was going to have to feel this one out.

Because of Alex's sudden appearance with her friends the night before, I hadn't gotten a chance to finish the tiny wedding cakes I'd planned for them. That was the first thing I got to work on after changing my shirt and splashing cold water on my face in the bathroom. Each one of the little cakes looked just like a real multi-tiered wedding cake, and I wanted to decorate each of them with buttercream and little fondant flowers and swags to keep up the appearance.

I hadn't asked for Gabriela's wedding colors, so I just went with basic pearl to create a classic all-white wedding cake look. I hadn't been able to choose between vanilla and chocolate cake, so each cake had both, with coffee-flavored buttercream in between the layers.

With those finished, I placed each on a plate with an airplane bottle of liquor and a chocolate cup filled with coffee-flavored mousse. Wrapping them carefully in plastic, I put them in the refrigerator with a note to give them to Alex and her friends if they stopped in. By now, my employees recognized Alex, so they would know when they saw her.

The next step in my early morning preparations was to finish the picnics for my customers who would be coming by later in the day to get them. I added the breadsticks and cheese straws, then sandwiches, crackers and cheese, and fruit tarts. Each one got a personalized name tag, and then they were placed in the larger refrigerator as well.

At this point, it was time to fill the display case and get ready to open up. I wasn't going to be able to stay at the shop long that morning. I had an appointment with a lawyer I'd contacted after Holly left all those messages, so it was going to be just my tiny staff handling the rush. I knew they could do it; they were both very good at what they did and had been involved with the shop for long enough to know it inside and out. But I was still so protective of the shop, my customers, and even them that I worried as I walked out and headed for my appointment. I didn't want anything to go wrong while I was trying to handle this craziness with Holly. She wanted to cause trouble, but I didn't want to give her that satisfaction.

Sitting across from the lawyer, Greg Phillips, in his office an hour later, I detailed everything that had happened with Holly. I gave him the full story of how I'd come to the decision to start The Coffee Shop, how I named it, where I got my menu items, and everything else I could possibly think of that might help him understand the situation fully.

"So, you see, she really had nothing to do with it. I know she's still really angry about the money and probably about our relationship ending, but that doesn't mean she's entitled to any part of my business or its profits," I said.

"You're right. It doesn't. From what I'm hearing from you, she had no participation in the development of the business and no bearing on the success it has experienced. That means she has no legal interest in any kind of profit share, partial ownership, control, job, or anything else having to do with it," he said.

"Good. That makes me feel better to hear," I said.

"Well," he said in a way I really never wanted to hear my lawyer say it, "us knowing that and it being a completely smooth experience in terms of court and anything else she might try to do are different things. She might be able to convince the judge that because you were in a long-term relationship, she obviously had some part in the building of the business. Or that you took care of her before and then broke up with her, and so you in essence robbed her of the potential life she could have led.

"There are definitely things I would recommend doing and ways we could handle this thing proactively rather than waiting for it to get worse. That's the thing. You have nothing to hide and nothing to be ashamed of. We just have to make sure that's the message and it's convincing."

I felt better but also a little worse leaving the lawyer's office. It was good to know he agreed with me and thought Holly had nothing to stand on. But it was a bit disconcerting that he could also see the potential of her causing me grief as this whole thing played out. We'd made another appointment to talk later, and I promised I'd keep him updated if anything else happened.

When I got back to work, I asked if Alex had gotten her cakes, trying subtly to find out if she had come by. Kristie told me no, and I felt a wave of disappointment, but it was the way it was. I'd just have to wait to find out where we stood.

Chapter Fifteen

Alexis

I was hoping to be able to sleep off the effects of the bachelorette party by the next morning, but that didn't happen. I woke up enough to say goodbye to the ladies as they headed home, but then fell right back to sleep. They should have just stayed here and made a weekend out of it, but Gabriela had wedding planning appointments, Valerie had a doctor's appointment, and the others had family obligations that were keeping them from just taking all the time off. I understood, but it would have been nice to just be able to hang out for the whole weekend like we used to when we were younger and didn't have children, husbands, and careers to think about.

Not that I'd want them to give up those things in their lives. I knew how much they meant to them. Tracy was an amazing stepmother to her husband's children. Sarah took care of her elderly grandparents and spent all her free time volunteering. They were the best kinds of obligations and I was proud of all my friends. But I also missed all the time we got to spend together.

And if I was being really honest with myself, I'd admit I was worried that time was only going to get less and less. I didn't want to say it to any of them, I barely even wanted to say it to myself, but there was a voice in the back of my head when I watched them with their families or heard them talking about all the amazing things they were doing, that said I was being left behind.

I didn't always feel that way. This was the path I'd chosen and exactly what I wanted in my life. The career I'd aspired to and was making better all the time. The home that was the dream I carried and the marker I'd placed in front of myself as what would tell me I'd finally made it. I was an adult and building my own life.

Those times didn't always drown out the ones of doubt, though. I still wondered what it was going to be like when Gabriela got married and Valerie had her baby and suddenly Sarah and I were the only ones unmarried and without children, and I was the only one without anything but myself. While my friends were creating their own little mommy and me groups and sharing couple dates, I wondered how I was going to fit in.

That Saturday after the bachelorette party, though, I didn't get a whole lot of time to dwell in those thoughts. I fell back to sleep after they left, only to be woken up a couple of hours later by a call from Gabriela.

She sounded absolutely frantic.

"Alex, I don't know what I'm going to do. What am I going to do?"

Sleep was still fogging my brain as I tried to figure out what she was talking about. I thought maybe she'd told me something and I'd just forgotten it.

"Gabriela? What's going on? What do you mean what are you going to do?" I asked.

"I need you. Can you come over right now?" she asked.

It was the second time in a week I'd been beckoned to one of my best friends' houses in that way, but I had a very strong feeling this was not going to be a relaxed evening of eating bizarre food combinations and debating the benefits of various parenting styles and whether she should allow both her mother and her mother-in-law in the birthing room with her.

Gabriela sounded on the brink of falling apart. Her voice was tight and tense, and I could hear tears in it. She wasn't one to cry easily.

Something serious must have happened to make her this emotional, especially if she wasn't willing to even talk to me about it over the phone. She had to have an in-person conversation.

I hoped there wasn't something wrong with her and Dean. They couldn't have cancelled the wedding. They were so in love and so excited about finally getting married. I didn't think there was any way in the last twenty-four hours they could have found a reason to break up. As I was rushing around trying to get myself presentable enough to actually go out in public, I thought about the night before. Bachelorette parties were notorious for being rowdy and filled with all kinds of poor decisions. I'd even known a couple of friends and family members who rethought their impending weddings because of things that happened at either the bachelorette or bachelor parties.

But nothing like that had happened at Gabriela's party. Right? I thought through it as carefully as I could, trying to go through every minute and everything we did. There was definitely some ridiculousness, but I couldn't think of anything that would spell doom for the couple. As far as I knew, the only one of us who had even close to that level of questionable behavior was me.

I cringed at the thought of Nick turning me down at the door the night before. That was just brutal. Not that he made the wrong decision. When I forced myself to look past my pride and bruised ego, I appreciated that he had been the adult in the situation and didn't take me up on my drunken offer to come inside with me. It wasn't completely alcohol-induced, but certainly alcohol-induced enough for him to have done the absolute right thing by saying no and walking away.

Pushing that out of my mind, I grabbed my keys and my phone and took off out of the building. I was still feeling the effects of the exhaustion from the night before, and my head was throbbing when I got behind the wheel, but I was sober, and I figured there would be some kind of caffeine and salt combination available at Gabriela's house to combat the hangover. I just had to get there. And that was a challenge in and of itself. I was dragging and several times just wanted to pull off on the side of the road, make camp, and head for the summit in the morning.

I wasn't cut out for partying like we were still in our early twenties. That made me feel ancient, but I would take feeling old over spending every weekend like this any time.

I finally made it to Gabriela's house, and she rushed outside before I was even out of the car. She threw her arms around me.

"It's a disaster," she said. "It's a complete disaster. I don't know what I'm going to do."

"Is it Dean?" I asked. "Did something happen between you two? Did you call off the wedding?"

She pulled back away from the hug and looked at me like I had lost my mind, which was probably warranted.

"No. It's not Dean. It's the food."

I blinked at her a couple of times. "The food?"

Gabriela let out a huge sigh and flounced her way back into the house. I locked my car with a little chipper beep-beep from my key fob that managed to make my head hurt more and followed her. Thankfully there was already a tray with coffee waiting on the table in the parlor, and I could smell food cooking in the kitchen.

I sat down and poured myself coffee, tipping it back despite the heat, then filling the cup again. Gabriela was pacing back and forth in front of me. She didn't look like she was feeling it anywhere near as much as I was. Granted, I didn't think she had downed nearly as many drinks the night before as I had. Pre-wedding panic might have also gone a good distance in mitigating the effects of the party.

"Remember when we were talking about my reception, and I told you all about my vision for the food and the cake?" she asked.

I nodded. "No sit-down dinner. Desserts and snacks and a big centerpiece cake."

It was a major simplification of her actual vision, which included elaborate dessert displays, themed snacks, and a towering cake that would take up essentially an entire table. I really liked the idea. I'd been too far more than enough weddings that included the stiff sit-down dinner that always looked and sounded better than it really was, or those of couples who thought they were being edgy by having action stations or buffets but were just the same as everyone else's who did the same thing.

The idea of being able to just enjoy the party with sweets and delicious finger foods sounded fantastic, and we'd been working on plans to give to the woman handling making the visions a reality for months. This close to the wedding, I figured everything had to be in place. All they should be doing at this point was finalizing details and sourcing ingredients.

Apparently not.

"Right. Which I thought was going to be so much easier and more fun for the caterer to do. And I didn't think for a second when my aunt told me that she wanted to handle all of it for me since she's friends with that chef. The one who just opened the totally vegan barbecue restaurant that has an exact plant-based replica menu as his conventional barbecue restaurant next door."

"I remember," I said.

"Well, it turns out, when she said she wanted to handle all of it for me," Gabriela said, the frantic tone in her voice starting to mix with a sarcastic, angry note, "she meant that she thought my idea was completely ridiculous and low-class and wanted to make the menu what she thought would be appropriate. She went behind my back and planned this whole absurd ten-course tasting menu with all kinds of strange food. No desserts because she says it's offensive to a chef to offer desserts after a meal.

"And then instead of giving the bakery my design and asking for the flavors I wanted, she ordered a tiny, plain white thing she called a 'ceremonial cake' because according to her, the only thing a wedding cake is good for is the ceremony of cutting it and then everybody getting one mouthful for tradition's sake."

"Oh, no," I said. "And you just found this out?"

She held up a finger and walked out of the room. When she came back a second later, she was carrying a platter full of the reason we were best friends. Extra buttered grilled cheese sandwiches and fries with a side of mayonnaise. The cure to all ills.

"Yes. This morning. My mother finally told me. My aunt has been saying she wanted everything a secret so it would be some wonderful surprise on my wedding day, but when my mother found out the details, she thought I should know," Gabriela said.

She set the food on the table in front of me, and I immediately grabbed for one of the fries, stuffed it in my mouth, then grabbed a sandwich triangle.

"Thank you so much." I took a bite. "Did you talk to your aunt?"

"I called her and asked what the hell she thought she was doing, and she got all offended because she couldn't understand how I wouldn't fall all over myself in appreciation for her 'fixing' my wedding and making sure it was the social event it was supposed to be rather than a glorified children's birthday party. She went on to say it would be offensive and embarrassing to the entire family for someone of my station to have a reception like that, and I needed to think about how this was going to look to everyone else."

"Funny, I thought it was your wedding," I said. "And that you were supposed to be creating a day that was important and meaningful to you and Dean."

"Yeah, I thought that, too. And when I told her that, she completely flew off the handle and told me that she's canceling everything. She's refusing to do anything to fix the situation, so now I have no food, no dessert, no cake. Nothing. My wedding is in a week. What am I going to do?"

That was when the tears started. They'd tried hard to hold back, but the situation was obviously overwhelming her, and I could absolutely understand why. This was ridiculous. I finished the bite of sandwich I was working on and got up to comfort her. She fell into my hug, crying and shaking her head.

"Everything is going to be fine. It's going to work out," I said.

"I'm going to have to order pizza," she said.

"No, you won't."

"Or fast food."

I laughed a little. "No. It's not going to get to that. I promise. We're going to find a solution. This is going to be fine, and you're going to have the exact wedding you dreamed of."

"Really?" she asked.

"Of course."

"So you're going to fix it for me?" she asked.

"What?" I asked.

She pulled back and looked at me with her tear-filled eyes. "You're going to fix it. You'll find a way to make this work, right? Be my maid of honor and rescue my wedding?"

I couldn't say no. I couldn't look at my best friend who was completely freaking out about her wedding going up in flames and tell her that there was nothing I could do about it.

Which is what led to me driving down the road with a plate full of grilled cheese and fries on the passenger seat beside me while I did my best not to freak out myself while searching every corner of my brain for the solution to this mess.

My first thought, of course, was Nick. He'd already swooped in to save me with food a couple of times. I was sure he had the ability to do it again. But I couldn't ask him. I didn't want to take advantage of him or make him feel like the only thing I thought he was good for was emergency food. Besides, I was still feeling a little strange about the kiss.

It was fantastic, but I couldn't shake the doubt running through the back of my head that said maybe he didn't want to kiss me. Maybe I really was totally misreading everything, and he just kissed me back because I threw myself at him and he couldn't escape. Was it possible I wasn't even remembering the kiss correctly at all? Could I have totally imagined him holding me the way he did and the way his lips moved across mine? I thought I'd gotten it together by that point, but maybe I'd just made it up because that was what I wanted to happen.

Is that what I wanted to happen? What did I want now? The whole thing was just awkward.

I spent the rest of the afternoon calling around to as many places as I could think of and stopping into others to try to find anyone who might be able to step up and fix this nonsense. It was only a week away, so even with the kind of budget Gabriela's father was willing to put down for the food, no one could even come close to fitting it in with the rest of their current schedule.

Finally, there were no other options left. I had to go to Nick.

He was cleaning up when I got to the door of the shop and knocked on it gently. One of the things that I did remember distinctly from the night before was pounding on the glass with a massive deficit of dignity, so I didn't want to reenact that situation. The light tapping was enough for him to look up and notice me. He came to the door and opened it, looking slightly surprised to see me.

"Hey, Alex," he said. "Come on in."

I stepped in, and he shut the door behind me.

"First, I want to say I'm sorry for last night. I shouldn't have come here and put you through all that. It was ...." I shook my head. "I'm sorry."

Nick laughed and went into the kitchen, then came back with what looked like a very tiny wedding cake and several miniature bottles of liquor.

"Don't worry about it. I understand." He set the cake on the counter. "Let me get you some coffee. I made these cakes for you ladies thinking you might need a bit of a pick-me-up after last night."

"Oh, my goodness, you are amazing," I said, grabbing a fork and diving into the cake before realizing what I'd said. "I mean... this is amazing. Thank you."

Nick smiled as he put the coffee in front of me. "How's your day been?"

Maybe I should have taken the opportunity to engage in some casual friendly small talk before dropping the hammer, but I didn't feel like I had the luxury of time at the moment, so I dove right in.

"Actually, this cake seems a little prophetic," I said.

His eyebrow raised, and I plunged ahead with the story.

"I know it's insane that I'm even asking you, and I'm so sorry to spring it on you..."

"Of course, I'll do it."

"I would totally understand if you said no, but...what?"

He smiled. "I said I'll do it."

"Are you serious?"

"Yes. But only if you'll help me," Nick said.

All the hope I'd felt for that brief second drained out of me. "Do you not remember the lemon bar situation?"

"I promise I'll only give you jobs you can handle," he said.

I didn't really have a choice. I stuffed more cake in my mouth, swallowed hard, and agreed.

Chapter Sixteen

Nick

Alex looked like me agreeing to help her with the wedding with the best news she had ever heard. Though it was a massive undertaking and I didn't actually know if I had the time or ability to pull off something like that, it wasn't in me to turn her down. As soon as she started talking about how upset her friend was and the awful way her aunt had let her down, I knew she was going to ask if I could help her. And I was going to say yes.

To be honest, even if she hadn't asked me to help and she had just shown up at the shop to vent and tell me how overwhelmed and worried she was about this new maid of honor responsibilities, I would have offered to take on the job for her. I hated to see so much worry and panic in Alex's eyes. I just wanted to make her feel better and let her know everything was going to work out. Even if that meant working nonstop for the next week.

But that was where telling her I needed her help was going to come in. Of course, I knew she had to work for part of the week. But she had already mentioned to me that she had taken vacation days for some of it so that she wouldn't be too stressed out the weekend of the wedding itself. She wanted it to be available for Gabriela if there were any last-minute maid of honor needs, and this definitely fit the bill. That meant she would at least have some time to come in and help with the shop or do some small parts of making the food.

I wasn't going to be able to trust her with constructing entire elements of the menu, that was for sure. But there were parts of every recipe she could help with, even if it meant just grabbing ingredients or taking things out of the oven. I was confident she could manage that. And when she wasn't doing those things, she could help out at the shop doing some of the basic stuff I did throughout each day so I could use that time to do this.

Though I knew she was feeling anxious, I actually found myself excited at the prospect of working on this wedding. And not just because it would give me the opportunity to spend some extra time with Alex. This would be the first event of this scale I'd ever handled. It was a challenge, and I'd always enjoyed putting challenges in front of myself and seeing if I was able to tackle them. Becoming a caterer wasn't something that was on my list of aspirations, but providing the kinds of food I already made and some specialty items for events seemed like a logical progression.

I went into the office and got some paper and a pen so I could start taking notes.

"Why don't you tell me as much as you can about what she wanted or what she was expecting from the other people? Anything specific she asked for. Whatever you can think of. I can't guarantee one hundred percent that I'm going to be able to recreate the menu exactly with the short time frame, but I'm going to do the best I possibly can," I said.

"Trust me, at this point, she's going to be thrilled to have anything available for her guests to eat. If they are even vaguely close to what she wanted when this all started, she will be over the moon," Alex said.

"Then let's make that happen for her."

We sat at the shop for the next couple of hours going over everything Alex could think of that she and Gabriela had talked about while they were planning her wedding food. It sounded like the bride had a very clear vision of what she wanted for her celebration, and it was far from the stuffy, formal production her aunt had tried to force on her.

Rather than a formal meal or even a buffet, she wanted snacks themed to the different places and memories that were important to her and her soon-to-be husband. She wanted tables filled with all kinds of indulgent treats and desserts so the guests could enjoy themselves mingling, eating, dancing, and drinking rather than sitting at pre-assigned tables struggling their way through small talk and hoping for the evening to end.

I spoke about that from experience. While I wouldn't really say that I hated weddings the way Alex had confided in me she did, I'd certainly been to my fair share of boring, unpleasant ones. These plans definitely made it sound like Gabriela wanted anything but that kind of feeling for her reception, and I wanted to give that to her.

"I wouldn't ever say this to Gabriela because I know she's totally freaking out about this whole situation and is really hurt and upset at what her aunt did to her, but I am actually glad her aunt got mad at her and is refusing to do anything for her," Alex said when we'd finished making a list of the places, memories, and experiences that Gabriela wanted to theme food after. "I know that sounds like I want her to be upset, but I really don't. It's just that if she never found out about it or she just gave in, she'd end up with a miserable reception that had absolutely nothing to do with her."

She was echoing my sentiments exactly and I smiled at her from over the rim of my own cup of coffee.

"And that should be the whole point," I said. "Weddings shouldn't be about the guests or fitting into some sort of mold. They should be welcoming and make people comfortable and happy, of course, but the most important thing they are is a celebration of the couple. The reception should be a reflection of them and a chance for them to celebrate, enjoy themselves, and have a fantastic time with the people who mean the most to them. I think food can absolutely do that. In fact, I think it's one of the most important parts of a reception."

"Exactly. No one wants to feel like they went to the ceremony and were then funneled into some random restaurant to eat afterward. As much as I don't like weddings, the one thing that can make it far more tolerable is when every detail reminds me of the couple and makes it feel like this really is a whole celebration of these people I care about," Alex said.

Our eyes met, and for a moment I was locked in on her, only able to focus on her sitting there so close to me, bent over the paper, talking so no one else could hear us. I could feel heat building between us, a tug that reminded me of the kiss after the bachelorette party. For a second, I thought about kissing her again. Then I stopped myself. We needed to focus right now.

"What are you doing tomorrow?" I asked.

"Nothing," she said.

"Great. Both of my employees will be here in the morning, so I can slip out for a while. Meet me down here first thing, and we'll get started," I said.

"Thank you," Alex said. "I know this is a huge thing, and I can't tell you how much I appreciate it."

"Thank me after you've done all the work," I said with a laugh. "Go get some rest. You're going to need it."

She headed up to her apartment, and I stayed at the shop a little longer to finish up before going home. The next day was going to be long and challenging, but so was the rest of the week. We just needed to put our heads down and get through it. At least I was getting a chance to do it alongside Alex.

Shopping for ingredients and other supplies took most of the next morning to accomplish. I brought Alex with me around the city, introducing her to various supply stores and specialty markets I used to source everything I needed for my shop and for special orders. There were some things I had to order that wouldn't be available until later in the week, but we could work around that. As long as I made a tight schedule and stuck to it, everything could get finished.

When we got back to the shop, I created a timeline of how everything needed to get handled, right down to the day of the wedding itself. Alex watched in amazement some moments, overwhelmed fear in others. I assured her it was going to work. We were going to accomplish it.

My next step was getting her behind the counter helping out with the customers. It would give me peace of mind knowing that they were being taken care of and everything was under control so I could spend my time getting recipes organized and get started on a few things that could be made in advance.

A few times throughout the afternoon, I stepped out of the kitchen to watch Alex in action. I wasn't sure how she was going to do jumping in to working behind the counter, but she didn't miss a beat. Her personality shone as she greeted people, filled coffee orders, and joked with customers. I even caught her trying to sneak bits of information about me out of my customers.

"All right now, no colluding behind my back," I said playfully as I walked up to Barry.

He and Alex had been leaning toward each other chatting away, and I just knew he was spilling everything he could about me. Alex laughed and shrugged, holding up her hands innocently.

"You two sure are a cute couple," Barry said. "Took you long enough to bring her out so we could meet her."

Alex blushed and turned away, busying herself with an order that didn't exist. I nudged Barry.

"We're not a couple," I told him.

He leaned in close to me. "Yet."

I didn't argue.

As I headed back to the kitchen, I glanced back at her, and our eyes met. My heart thudded hard in my chest, and heat rolled along the back of my neck, settling in my belly. I had no doubts now about my feelings for her. I just hoped she was feeling the same. Right now wasn't the time to try to talk about it, but when all this wedding craziness was over, I wasn't going to hesitate anymore.

After the shop closed, Alex and I met up in the seating area at the front of the shop to keep working on the wedding. I told her about everything that I'd done during the day and briefed her on what we were going to work on the next day.

"Oh," she said after a few minutes, "I almost forgot to tell you. Some guy came in looking for you. Barry told him you were busy."

"Wearing a suit, carrying a briefcase, and looking like his phone was permanently affixed to his head?" I asked.

"Yeah," she said. "A friend of yours?"

"Not exactly. He's a business investor. He's been trying to convince me to sell the shop to him."

Her eyebrows raised. "Seriously?"

"Yep. He does not want to take no for an answer. He's come in a few times already, and it looks like he's doubling down on his frequency hoping he can just wear me down."

"Does that happen a lot?" she asked.

"I don't really know how much it happens to other people, so I can't say whether it's a lot of not, but it's a couple of times a month. There are other people who are trying to get me to franchise. They talk about opening other locations and packaging food and all kinds of things."

"It doesn't sound like that's something you're interested in," Alex said.

"I'm not. I'm happy with what I have. This shop was my dream, I accomplished it, now I want to make it the very best it can possibly be. I want to focus on my customers and try new things when I want to. I don't want to have to spread myself thin or answer to investors or see anything with my name and brand on it that isn't exactly the way I'd have it. That's just not the point of having this place," I said.

"I understand that," she said.

I laughed. "Besides, they're just assuming I'm crazy successful. If they got a look at my books, they might not think so. I handle them myself, and they are probably a total mess, to be honest. I don't even know if I'm doing them right. I think I am. The government hasn't come after me. But I don't know if I've done everything as efficiently as I should. And I feel like I need to revamp my budget and things now that I'm in a different place than I was at the beginning."

Alex looked at me like she was stunned at what she was hearing. I realized I'd probably made myself sound like a total idiot.

"Are you serious?" she asked.

"It's probably not as bad as all that," I said. "I just should have thought about having a professional do those things."

"Let me look at them," she said. I looked at her strangely, and she nodded. "That's what I do. That's my career. I went to school for accounting, and my job is all about handling the finances and investments of businesses to maximize their potential and set them up for future growth. I can look them over for you."

I shook my head. "No. I don't want to take advantage of you like that."

She cocked her eyebrow at me. "Am I taking advantage of you?"

"No, but..."

"Then let me do this for you. You are helping me so much. And at least this isn't something I can catch on fire." I looked at her with raised eyebrows. "Oh, yes. Consider that a disclaimer."

I laughed. "All right. You want to do it now?"

She nodded, and I gestured for her to follow me. "I'll show you the office."

Chapter Seventeen

Alexis

I sat down in Nick's office and started going over his finances. I was immediately engrossed and barely noticed when he came in with a glass of lemonade and a plate of special snacks for me. I continued browsing through his expenses and logs, and after a few minutes, I absently reached over and grabbed one of the little bites on the plate. Popping it in my mouth, I stopped when I tasted how delicious it was.

"What was that?" I asked.

He grinned at me. "That's one of the snacks I'm making for the wedding. It's a twist on spanakopita."

"It's amazing," I said, taking another and eating it. I sipped the lemonade to wash it down. "You know what else is amazing?"

"What?" he asked.

"Your books," I said.

"Amazing in how badly I managed to maintain them while keeping my shop open and myself out of federal prison?" he asked.

I laughed and shook my head. "No. You've actually done a really good job with it. I would never recommend a business owner who doesn't have a financial background try to handle their own books, but you've done really well. Better than some of my colleagues could do, actually. What I was saying is that the shop is really successful. Like, possibly more successful than I think you realize. And the potential is absolutely phenomenal.

"You could just go ahead and buy the whole building and be my landlord within the next year or two if you wanted. You know, you really might want to consider those franchising offers. You could get a lot just the rights for somebody else to open something that replicated this place. And you would be able to bring in a good steady income on a monthly basis if you structured the agreement correctly."

"No. I already told you. That's not something I even want to think about. I'm happy with my shop. I like my customers. I like being able to open when I want to enclose when I want to and not have people comparing this place to another one that has the same name but might not be the same quality. I don't want things to be more confusing. I'm already busy enough with work. I don't want to get so overwhelmed I'm not able to do the other things I want to do, like my volunteering," he said.

That comment stood out to me. I hadn't heard him say anything about any type of volunteer work.

"What type of volunteering?" I asked.

"There's a shelter and community center not far from here. I bring them food that's left over at the end of the day and make them some extra things when I know they have a lot of families or there are special occasions. And once a month, I go in and spend a day or two with them helping out, cooking, cleaning, repairs, hanging out with the people there. Whatever they need."

"That's amazing," I said. "I had no idea you did that."

Nick shrugged modestly. "It's not something I talk about, really. It's just something I do because I want to. I like being able to do something for other people when they need it. There were times when I was younger when I would have benefitted a lot from the kinds of services they offer, so I want to be able to support them giving those services to these families as much as possible."

I was blown away, and the tug I was feeling toward Nick only got stronger. I knew he was a good guy, and the fact that he gave of his time and effort so freely and enthusiastically just proved it even more.

"That's something you should talk about. You should tell people about it. I didn't even know there was a shelter and community center around here. I bet there are a lot of others who don't, either. But if you talked about it, maybe more people would get involved. You were saying that TV channels have approached you about doing features. Take them up on it and bring them to the shelter. Talk about your volunteering. It will highlight their services and also do great things for you," I said.

Nick was shaking his head before I even finished talking.

"No. That's not why I do it. I don't want any of the attention. I don't want it to become something about me. I do it because I want to help the center. Not for any other reason."

I could tell this was something that meant a lot to him, so I backed off.

"Hey. I think both of us need a break from all this wedding stuff and baking and finances and everything. What do you think about going out and actually doing something?" I suggested.

"Like what?" he asked.

"I don't know. What would you want to do?" I asked.

"Well, I am kind of hungry and would like to eat something I didn't make here in the shop," he said.

I laughed. "All right. What do you want? You pick."

Nick looked like he was thinking over the decision very carefully for a few seconds, then gave a single, affirmative nod.

"Pizza."

Somehow, that was not what I was expecting, and yet it seemed exactly right.

"All right," I said with another laugh. "Pizza it is. There's a place up the street I ordered from when I was moving. It was pretty good. Want to order some?"

"Even better. There's an old school pizza parlor a few streets over that I love. It's been in the same family for generations, and they use recipes from way back. Homemade dough, sauce, the whole thing. But the kids have started adding their own spin on things, too, so there's a whole section of the menu with their own combinations of toppings and add-ons and things. It's the best pizza you'll ever have," he said.

"Let's go," I agreed.

It turned out, Nick knew his pizza. I probably should have expected that. I wasn't going to go with the old cliché and say he was a bachelor without someone at home to cook for him so he probably subsisted on pizza and takeout. I knew his skills well enough at this point to be confident he probably did his fair share of cooking at home. But he didn't skimp on knowing his local foodie gems, either. The parlor was just as he described it: old, small, and incredibly nostalgic. It was also the absolute best bite of pizza I'd ever put in my mouth.

We spent an hour there laughing over stories from our childhood and our reactions to different flavor combinations we ordered on individual slices rather than getting one big pie. In the end, we both decided we were far too traditional in our pizza tastes for some of the ingredients the youngest generation of the family had introduced onto the menu, preferring pepperoni, pineapple, and onion. Maybe a bit of black olive if we were feeling really wild.

"All right, your turn," Nick said when we were finished and walking out of the shop.

"My turn?" I said.

"Yep. You decide what's next."

"I am stuffed. I couldn't possibly eat anything else," I said.

He grinned. "It doesn't have to be eating. I just want to spend more time with you."

Heat burned on my cheeks, and I couldn't help the huge grin that crossed my lips.

"Oh. Okay. Well, there is something I've been wanting to try but haven't been able to get any of my friends to go with me," I said.

Nick raised an eyebrow at me. "I'm intrigued."

I smiled. "It's across town, so we're going to have to drive."

He gestured ahead. "Lead the way."

I drove us across town to the area populated with more entertainment venues, shops, and restaurants than residential buildings. We parked in a parking deck and walked a couple of blocks to an indoor adventure park I'd seen being advertised for months since they opened.

"A lot of what they do is birthday parties and play groups for kids, obviously, but they've been advertising their glow nights for adults, and it sounded like a blast. Valerie can't exactly do any of the activities, obviously, and it's just not Gabriela's thing. No one has wanted to come try it out. What do you think?" I asked.

Nick watched a group of people go inside, the open door letting loud music flow out onto the sidewalk. I was feeling slightly ridiculous about the suggestion and about to withdraw it when a smile brightened his whole face.

"Let's do this."

My heart jumped, and I nearly squealed with excitement as we rushed in. We went up to the ticket counter and looked up at a large board displaying all the different options for activities and ticket levels. Without even looking at each other, we both told the young guy behind the register that we wanted the ultimate option, giving us access to every activity and room within the building.

He nodded his apparent approval, took our payment, and handed us glow sticks.

"It's dark in there, so make sure you're wearing these at all times. Shoes are required on the ropes course, no shoes allowed in the foam pits. Have fun," he told us.

Nick and I took off running through the black swinging doors that blocked the lobby area from the actual activity space. We slowed down only for a second when we heard the employee shouting after us not to run, then scurried toward the nearest activity, a ropes course that towered high above the rest of the floor.

There was something exhilarating about the silliness, about feeling like we were teenagers breaking rules just to push the boundaries. Scrambling up toward the ceiling and crossing obstacles I could barely see was frightening, but the adrenaline sent a thrill through me. I knew the harness would hold me up, and I also knew Nick was close behind me. I could feel his body there, sometimes just inches away as we moved through the various platforms and bridges.

When we finished that, we took off our shoes and jumped into a giant pit full of foam blocks that reminded me of gymnastics classes when I was young. The glow sticks we were wearing gave off just enough light that I was able to see Nick and was aware of little bits of illumination from other people around us, but I couldn't actually see them. It was like it was just the two of us. We laughed as we tossed blocks at each other and tried to swim around, then made our way toward large, cushioned balance beams where we could test out our American Gladiator skills, battling it out with massive, cushioned sticks.

The hours spent at the park released the tension and stress that had built up with the pressure of the wedding and gave us a chance to just relax and have fun. Being so active felt good, and I didn't mind all the times during the night when I found myself wrapped in Nick's arms as he playfully tossed me into the foam or pushed past me trying to win the obstacle course.

Finally, it was time to head home. There was still so much to be done, and we needed to not be completely exhausted when it was time to do it the next day. Nick insisted on walking me to my apartment when we got back, and I didn't argue. We stopped outside the door and looked at each other for an intense moment.

I was hot and sweaty, but I didn't care. When he leaned forward to kiss me, I melted into him. The kiss was hot and deep, one of his hands gripping me tightly against him while the other dug into my hair like he was holding me in place. I held tightly to his shoulders and pressed my body against his, wanting to find as much of his warmth as I could.

The kiss ignited me on the inside, but I stopped myself from inviting him in again. It didn't go so great for me the last time, and I didn't want to go for that humiliation twice in a row. I would just wait and see where this went.

Chapter Eighteen

Nick

A couple of days later, I did something I had never done since opening the shop. I stayed closed for the day. It wasn't because I didn't want to see my customers or because I didn't feel like being there. That was one of the days when my employees weren't scheduled to come in, and I knew if I was going to get everything that needed to be done for the wedding finished in time, I needed as much time to focus on it as I possibly could. So I kept the closed sign up and left a note saying I'd be back to regular business hours soon.

I also made sure I had the coffeemakers going and a stash of some of the favorites of my regular customers, like Barry, so if they came by, I'd still be able to give them something to go. Just as I had expected it to be, tackling this massive undertaking with such a short timeline was hard. So far, I had managed to keep to my schedule and get everything done the way I'd hoped, but I was starting to get nervous that everything wasn't going to keep going as smoothly as it had been so far.

A couple of the special ingredients that I had to order hadn't come when they were supposed to early that morning, and I was waiting nervously to see if they would get there by the afternoon. If they arrived at least within a few hours of when they were originally scheduled to, I would still be able to rearrange the order of things to make it all fit. The situation was getting a bit tenser, but it was worth the stress. Especially because I knew Alex was coming in that evening to help.

After taking two days off, she had to return to the office, so I hadn't seen her the day before. I only got a quick hello and good morning with her that day when she stopped in to grab coffee and a pastry before heading to work. I would happily take those short bits of time with her if they were all I could get, but the promise of much more time with her that evening was keeping my mood high and my motivation going as I worked. I looked forward to being able to show her all my progress to keep her at ease that the wedding was going to be perfect that weekend.

Partway through the afternoon, I noticed Barry standing at the outside door, staring at the sign like he just couldn't understand what it said. His routine was being thrown off, and that was just not acceptable for him. I'd planned on just handing him his coffee and the food I'd made with him in mind through the door, but his arrival came just as I was feeling like I needed to take a bit of a break myself. I went to the door and opened it, inviting him in.

I would have rather sat on the couch, but Barry was already not happy about the shop being closed when it should have been open and wasn't going to compromise on sitting in his usual spot. I sat on the stool beside him and tucked into a sandwich and cup of extra-strong coffee.

"What's going on?" he asked. "Why aren't you open?"

He sounded nervous, like he was waiting for me to drop some sort of terrible news on him. I quickly explained the wedding and all the work I was trying to get done in time. He looked relieved as he ate a miniature bacon and onion quiche.

"Alex," he said almost like he was trying out the name. He nodded. "That's that girl who was here a couple days ago. She was messing up coffee orders and smiling at people so they didn't notice."

I laughed. If he was right, which I was sure he was because Barry didn't miss a thing, she had certainly been doing a good job with those smiles because I hadn't noticed a single upset customer or wrong order. Maybe if it had been someone else, I would have noticed. But that day, all I noticed was Alex.

"That's her," I said.

"You two a couple yet?" he asked without hesitation or pretense. He didn't care if he was asking something that might seem inappropriate or prying to some people. He was just going to put it right out there. It didn't bother me. In fact, it gave me the chance to talk things through with him.

"No," I said. "But I think I want to be."

His eyebrows lifted. "Oh?"

"Yeah. I've told you about my ex. You know how all that went down. And things are getting messy with her again for a whole new set of reasons. And it's because of all that I didn't think I wanted to get anywhere near having someone in my life for a good while. It's just too complicated. And, frankly, it didn't seem worth it."

"Until you met Alex," Barry said.

"Until I met Alex. There's just something about her. I don't even know how to explain it. Everything I could say about her sounds cliché and ridiculous. Like I could sit here and say she's beautiful and funny and kind and ambitious and loves her friends. And it sounds like I'm just rattling off the same words that everybody says about people. They've been said so much they don't really even mean anything. But they're true. And yet, that's not enough. There's something else, and I can't put words to it, but I can't get enough of it.

"I thought it might just be a crush, just an attraction because she is gorgeous and new, but that's not what this is. My feelings are getting really real. I think I might be ready to try another go at a relationship. She seems like the perfect fit."

It was good, if not a little intimidating, expressing that out loud. Feeling this way was big for me. I hadn't even had a second thought about dating since Holly, and I figured it was just going to be that way into the future. I hoped I wasn't going to end up being like one of those old sea captains who described the sea as their lady. I really didn't want coffee to be my lady. But at the same time, I didn't want to go through any of the stress and drama of a bad relationship again, either.

The friendship I'd built with Alex and the strong feelings that were coming from it were the first time in years I'd thought there could be more. It was exciting, and I was really looking forward to after the wedding when I could see where things could go when we were able to focus just on us.

Later that evening, Alex was following after me as I piped pate a choux on silicone baking mats, using a wet finger to gently tamp down the tips left behind so they didn't burn when they were baking. These would eventually be filled with several different flavors of cream and coated with chocolate or vanilla for the dessert table. We'd been talking about her day, and I filled her in on all of the Banana Split updates from Barry.

"I talked to Gabriela earlier today," she said. "She can't believe how much you've done."

"You didn't tell her everything, did you?" I asked.

"No. I kept the surprises we planned," she said.

"Good. I'm glad I get to be there to set everything up so I can see how she reacts," I said.

Alex seemed to think about this for a second.

"You know, Gabriela doesn't just think of you as the person making the food. You're obviously doing that, and I know you're going to have a lot to do on that day, but she also thinks of you as a guest."

"She does?" I asked.

"Of course, she does. So I was thinking, maybe you should also be my date."

She looked up at me, and somehow the tiny hint of nervousness in her eyes, like she really thought there was a chance I was going to say no to her, made her even more adorable. I grinned.

"I would love to be your date. And to have you as mine," I said.

Alex smiled, and I went back to piping cream puffs feeling happier than I had in a long time.

A little while later, Alex had to leave to tend to some bridesmaid duties, but she didn't walk out of the shop without first giving me a soft kiss. She started to walk away, and I tugged her back for one more, making her giggle as she finally left.

I was still thinking about that kiss when my phone rang. It was soon enough after Alex left that I thought it might be her, but my mood dropped a bit when I saw it was actually Holly. I wanted to ignore her. But I knew if I didn't answer, she was just going to keep calling, fill up my voicemail box with messages, and possibly eventually decide to just show up at the shop. She would do anything to get the attention she wanted, just the way she always did, and the last thing I wanted was to have to deal with her in person.

I would just deal with a phone call, get it over with, and go about my day.

"What do you want, Holly?" I answered.

"Well, that's rude," she said.

I didn't want to let her bring down my mood completely. I didn't want to let her ruin the happy feeling I was finally getting to enjoy on a regular basis. But she made that very difficult. This woman had a knack for creating misery and testing even the most stable of tempers.

"Rude?" I asked. "I'm the one being rude? Did you hear yourself leaving any of those phone messages?"

"I was perfectly civil with you in those messages, and I probably shouldn't have been. You know who I heard from today? Your lawyer. I can't believe you. I can't believe you seriously went and hired a lawyer. You are being so aggressive about this. You just want to continue to punish me for the end of our relationship."

Holly sounded furious, but I couldn't help but scoff at that sentiment.

"I'm not punishing you for anything, Holly. The fact that our relationship ended has no impact on my life now. It was a long time ago, and I consider it a part of my distant history," I said.

"That is so like you, being so cruel. I guess I should expect nothing less from you. You know I'm right about this, Nick. You are the one who destroyed what we had. I was entitled to some of the money from your mother," she said.

There was another half of that comment, but I didn't let it come out of her mouth.

"Don't you dare talk about her. I don't know what possessed you to think that, but you in no way had any claim to anything having to do with my mother. That was my inheritance, intended for me, and to be used as I saw fit. You didn't have any claim to any of it. You were not my wife. At any point."

She gasped, but it sounded affected, and I wondered if she was recording the conversation. I needed to be very careful about what I said just in case she was. I didn't put it past her to try to doctor anything I said to manipulate other people into thinking what she wanted them to, or to convince me to do what she said.

"You're going to throw that in my face? When I was devoted to you for three years? You have always been so selfish, but you've gotten truly horrible. I never wanted to believe you were going to be like this, even though people warned me. I should have put things in writing. I should have done something to show that I am the one who suggested the name The Coffee Shop. I inspired half of the treats on your menu. And you don't think I deserve even the smallest recognition."

"None of that is true," I said as calmly as I could, trying not to engage her any further.

"It is. And you know it is. I was the heart and soul of your life, the thing that gave you the strength to get as far as you have, and you have just tossed me away. I'm not even asking much. Nowhere near as much as I actually deserve. I think it is the absolute least you can do to start another location so that I can take over the one in the Bentley."

"What?" I said, the word exploding out of me. "You can't possibly be serious."

"You know it's been my dream for years to live there. And running the shop would make everything so much more convenient and let me afford the apartment. I don't understand why it matters so much to you to be there. You don't even live in the building. Another location would be making money immediately. That one is doing super well. Grayson told me it's always crowded."

Spots danced in front of my eyes, and I had to take a second before answering.

"Grayson? The building tour guide?"

"He's a concierge and resident liaison," she corrected as if that meant a damn thing. "Yes. He and I shared a very special night, and he told me all about the shop."

Disgusted didn't even begin to describe how I was feeling about this whole situation. I didn't care that she was seeing other people or how many beds she hopped into. It really didn't matter to me. It was her life, and she could do whatever she wanted to do. But I found it revolting that she'd ended up with the sleazy tour guide, and their pillow talk was all about my shop.

Even more than that, I was just infuriated and sickened that Holly was so selfish and oblivious that she would even think for a second I would give up what I'd worked so hard to build. Or that I was stupid enough to hand her a successful business so she could move into a luxury apartment and run off with that guy.

"Absolutely not. You're delusional if you think that's even close to something that would ever happen. You need to leave me alone before I escalate my lawyer's involvement," I said.

"You better think hard before you make any more bad decisions, Nick," she said, all pretend innocence gone from her voice. "I won't be finished until I get what's mine."

Chapter Nineteen

Alexis

My phone chimed, and I laughed when I saw another text message from Nick. He had been sending me messages and pictures throughout the day, keeping me updated on his progress as we went down the home stretch toward the wedding. Some of the pictures were just of the desserts and snacks, making my stomach rumble and, not for the first time, amazing me with what he was capable of doing.

This picture, though, wasn't of something he was crafting for Gabriela. Instead, it was a small white baker's box with a clear plastic window, a batch of lemon bars visible inside. Around the box looked like a glass display case, and I recognized both as being the boutique gift shop where I'd purchased the original lemon bars to thank him for helping me move.

Fresh out of the oven he'd captioned the picture.

Be careful, don't burn yourself, I wrote back. *You might want to use an oven mitt*

He sent back a laughing face, and I typed in a heart. I hesitated for a second. Was I really the kind of woman to send a heart emoticon through a text message to a grown man? A grown man who I wasn't even officially dating unless it was fair to count the wedding? I erased the heart and sent back a laughing face instead.

I went back to work, and a few moments later my phone alerted again. I smiled as I picked it up, looking forward to seeing what he was sending me this time. Instead, what I got was a reminder from my mother that we were supposed to meet for lunch. I let out a sigh and sent back a message telling her I hadn't forgotten, and I'd meet her at the restaurant in an hour just like we'd planned. She'd probably message me a couple more times before I actually saw her, convinced I couldn't keep up with the schedule.

I actually made it to the restaurant before she did but didn't bother to mention it when she swept in, reminding me of a bird that had just gotten swept up in a brief gust of wind. She'd likely just take that as an opportunity to point out I hadn't, in fact, known when I was supposed to be there and had instead arrived early rather than on time. Punctuality was a sticking point for my mother. Anyone in the family could tell you that the more stressed and flustered my mother got, the more stringent she got about social etiquette. It was like she created a shield around herself with propriety and adherence to cultural mores.

"How are you?" I asked, standing as she approached the table.

She gave me a quick hug and an air kiss in the direction of my cheek. Public displays of affection, even toward your children, were never acceptable. At least not when she was a couple of days away from a major social event like Gabriela's wedding, which she was managing to treat like it was for her own daughter. She'd done enough fretting and worrying to release all female members of Gabriela's family from such responsibilities leading up to and possibly even on the day of the wedding.

"My dress isn't ready yet. Can you believe that? I specifically told the tailor I needed it in plenty of time to make sure that my makeup artist could see the color and use it to finalize my makeup look for the day. It was supposed to be in two days ago, and it still hasn't been finished. She won't even answer my calls. I don't know what I'm going to do."

"Mom, the wedding isn't until this weekend. You still have time. And people are going to be paying far more attention to the bride and her parents," I said.

She glared at me. "What's that supposed to mean?"

I sighed and sipped my water. I knew I shouldn't have said that. But it was starting to get to me how much my mother was throwing herself into this wedding. I understood how much she cared about Gabriela. We'd been friends a very long time, and my mother had developed a great affection for her, so it made sense she would care about her wedding. But it felt like she was taking it just a bit too far. Like she was using up all the emotion she should have for my wedding on this one. Almost as though she'd given up on the idea of actually being the mother of the bride.

"Nothing."

She stared at me for a second, then turned her attention to the menu in front of me.

"At least all the decision-making was done for you when it comes to what you're wearing," she said. "That's one of things that makes it so nice to be a bridesmaid. You know you'll look lovely, and you don't even have to choose what you're going to wear."

"That's not really the sentiment most people have, Mom," I said. "There's a reason why the ugly bridesmaid dress is a trope. And a lot of brides these days let their bridesmaids choose their dress. They just pick a color or two and let them do whatever they want."

She didn't even look up from the menu. It was like she was blocking those words from going into her brain and she wasn't going to process them. That was just too much for her.

"One thing I wish you had chosen is a date," she said. "It's just going to be so awkward with you as maid of honor without someone to escort you during the reception. There aren't any single groomsmen. Dr. Maynard is going to be there with his family, though. His sweet son was so excited to surprise you. I don't understand why you two haven't made things official yet. If you're playing hard to get, I commend you, but I think you've taken it far enough."

"I have a date," I threw into the very brief space of her taking a breath before she sealed the plan of setting me up for the wedding with Trevor.

I haven't seen or spoken with Trevor since he'd shown up at my building, but apparently he told everyone we'd had a lovely reunion and he was really looking forward to spending more time with me soon. I wasn't sure if he was saying that only to save face or if he truly didn't grasp what had happened between us. What happened between us that day and every other time we saw each other.

But at least him saying that had saved me from having to hear all about my rudeness from my mother.

"You do?" Mom asked, sounding incredulous. "Who? Why haven't I heard anything about this?"

"It's no one you know," I said. "I don't want you to turn it into a big thing."

I hadn't mentioned Nick, and I didn't want to go into any further detail with Mom. It felt like if I told her about him, it would be like putting too much emphasis on it, making it too real. I didn't want to put too much thought into the growing feelings I was experiencing for him. I just wanted to let things happen if they were going to. I didn't want to get hurt.

I steered the conversation away from my wedding date and instead let her tell me about Gabriela's honeymoon even though she'd already told me about it a dozen times, and I'd helped plan it. At least it kept the conversation to only veiled barbs at my lack of a partner and her apparently growing doubt that I'd ever go on a honeymoon of my own.

As I usually did, I left lunch feeling a bit aggravated and even more determined to keep striving for my own personal success. I wouldn't let her tell me who or what to be, or how I was going to define success and satisfaction in my life. At the same time, I found myself thinking about what it would be like to introduce Nick to my family and see their re-action.

Back at work, I enjoyed another hour of continuous messages and updates from Nick, even receiving an extremely dramatic video clip featuring sweeping shots of completed desserts and the progressing stages of the cake against a backdrop of swelling epic music.

I headed into the lounge for some water, trying to come up with my own video I could send back to him. As I was filling my bottle from the filter, I overheard some of my coworkers at a table talking. One of them mentioned a company they were working for giving back to the community through food drives every Thanksgiving and an Easter egg hunt in the spring. Another said theirs planned awareness runs throughout the year as well as donating to several organizations.

I walked over to the table.

"What are you talking about?" I asked.

"Oh, hey, Alex," one of the guys said. "We were talking about the Hometown Hero feature on the news. Have you seen it?"

I shook my head. "No. What is it?"

"The evening news has a segment called Hometown Hero. It highlights a specific business that is doing big things to make a difference in their community. They want to promote local businesses and the people who are behind them. It's a fantastic opportunity to get some visibility and a reputation boost. A lot of the companies we handle do charity work during the year. Fundraising, toy drives, food drives, blood drives, park cleanups, building, volunteering at events, donations. All kinds of things."

"That's fantastic," I said. "It's a great idea."

"Well, if any of your clients are doing anything noteworthy, let us know. The news channel has space for one more company."

"I think I might know of somebody," I said before I even thought it all the way through.

Part of me said I should talk to Nick before I did this, but I didn't have the time to waste. Besides, it was such a phenomenal chance to do great things for the business and for the community. It felt like the universe was speaking to me, giving me the perfect opportunity, so I decided to jump on it.

Chapter Twenty

Nick

"Oh, Nicky, you don't have to do that," Constance said as I picked up the dropped sandwich from the floor.

"I know," I said, grinning.

"I'm just as spry as ever, young man," she said with a false bravado. "I could have gotten it."

"I'm sure," I said. "At any rate, I've got it."

I kept moving, passing by her and into the back. It was my monthly volunteer day at the shelter, and I was feeling pretty good. Truthfully, I always felt good at the shelter. I enjoyed the work, I enjoyed the fact that it was service and not for profit, and I loved the company. The little old ladies who I worked with treated me like I was their grandson.

The shelter was operated by Betty and Constance, but mostly Betty. She was an ornery old woman, constantly bossing others around and making sure that everyone knew she was in charge. She was always sweet with me, though, constantly trying to feed me with candy she brought in and had stuffed in the deep recesses of her pocketbook. I was convinced that every grandmother had a pocketbook that was secretly a vortex to another dimension. You could fit a black hole in one.

Betty was now sitting in the office, going over the paperwork that she tended to do whenever things got overwhelmingly busy, like now. She knew she wasn't terribly great with crowds, and though her heart told her to operate a shelter and she was fantastic at making a lot out of a little, she knew she wasn't the best person to be the face of it. Hence Constance, tooling around at seventy-four years old like she was still in her teens at a roller skate drive-thru.

I liked doing everything I could to help the shelter, bringing in food and treats that would either go to waste or I made specifically for the event. I tended not to have too many things left over from day to day, but what I did have left from the day before my volunteer day went with me, along with the majority of what I would have worked on that day as well.

Today had been a host of sandwiches, cupcakes and cookies, along with a couple different cakes. Betty was in the back now with two slices of the carrot cake, which I made specifically for her and Constance.

It was almost like going home. I didn't have any family left, and these little old ladies were willing to step in and play mother and grandmother to me. Most of their families were off doing their own thing somewhere, and the adoption process had been quick. I was very quickly dubbed 'Nicky' or 'Baby' for those who had trouble remembering names.

I didn't mind. I loved those women. And I wanted to have both their energy and their dedication or service when I was their age.

"So what are you up to this weekend, Nicky?" Constance said as she circled back to me as I went behind the counter to start doling out the cupcakes for the dessert bar. "Anything fun and interesting I can live vicariously through you with?"

"Funny you should ask," I said. "I'm going to a wedding."

"Oh," came several excited voices that I wasn't aware were listening in. Over the counter popped the faces of Miss Mary, Bernita, Essy, and the one we just called Nanny. She was actually younger than the rest, only in her mid-sixties, but she had somehow gained the stature of being the motherly figure to all the other motherly figures.

"I love weddings," Miss Mary said. "They always remind me of my Greg."

"I love them too," Bernita said. "The dresses, the suits, the pomp and circumstance of it all."

"I rather enjoyed them myself," Essy said. "Always got laid, that's for sure."

"Essy!" Constance said in a laughing whisper-shout.

"What?" Essy said. "I might be old, but I'm not dead. I miss having a man take me out back and…"

"Would you stop it?" Bernita said, looking like she might faint. "I swear, Essy, the devil got into you young, and he never let go."

"Thank goodness," Essy cackled.

"Anyway," Constance said, looking over at me and ignoring the geriatric lady Casanova, "do you have a date?"

There was an expectant feeling in the air as they waited on me to respond. These ladies were always asking me if I had found a good girl to settle down with yet. Or, in Bernita's very open-minded case, 'if I had a boy, because that would be fine too, as it were.' But I had always been very clear to tell them that not only wasn't there one, but there were no prospects. I was simply too busy.

"Well, see, that's the funny thing," I said.

The following sound was complex and layered. It was both a sound of inhaling shock as well as squeals of expectant joy, mixed with various pitches of ravenous desire for gossip.

"Who's the lucky girl?" Constance asked. "Have you been dating long? Is she from in town?"

"Is she one of those girls from the theater? I saw them looking at you the other day when you were walking around town. Back when I was an actress, you better believe I would have chased after a boy as handsome as you are," Miss Mary said.

"No, no, no," I said, waving them off and accidentally flicking a little icing onto the box. Essy quickly took the opportunity to swipe her index finger through it and give it a taste.

"Seriously?" I laughed.

Essy shrugged.

"It's not on a cupcake anymore," she said. "Free game."

"Disgusting," Miss Mary commented.

"What's going on out here?" Betty asked, coming into the area and finding the gaggle of older women.

"Our Nicky has a date!" Constance said.

"Who is it?" Bernita asked, getting back to the point, despite my hope that Essy's finger-licking had drawn them off it.

"It's Alex," I sighed. "I'm just going as a friend."

"Alex?" Bernita asked with a sly grin.

"A friend," Miss Mary snickered.

"You sure have been talking about her a lot recently," Bernita continued.

"That you have," Constance said. "Maybe you ought to bring her around to help sometime. Let us get to know her."

"I bet she has her claws sunk in there good and tight, doesn't she, Nicky?" Miss Mary asked with a sigh. "Ah, young love. I miss being courted by a boy. Not that I don't love my Georgie, of course."

"No one doubts that," Betty said, rolling her eyes. "I swear, you two are still celebrating your first anniversary, fifty years later."

"It's wonderful, isn't it?" Nanny asked.

"It's nauseating," Betty said. "Men aren't any good after fifty. No offense, Nicky."

I laughed.

"So are you two an item yet?" Bernita said, doggedly continuing to keep the conversation on track.

"Not exactly," I laughed.

I stopped short before I went any further as the bell over the door sounded, and we all looked to see who was coming in. To my shock, and as if speaking her name had conjured her out of nothingness, it was Alex. She was standing in the doorway, looking around the room for me.

"Excuse me, ladies," I said. "That's her."

"Oh, my word," Miss Mary said. "She's perfect!"

"Did you see the smile on that boy's face?" Nanny asked. "He's got it bad, he does."

"Oh, will you stop?" Betty said. "He just said they are friends."

"Like you and William Frasier?" Constance asked to a chorus of gossipy laughter.

I could hear them chittering behind me as I excitedly made my way to Alex. She still had one foot propping the door open, like she was ready to run out at a moment's notice if she didn't see me. But when our eyes met, she smiled brightly, letting the door shut behind her, and I felt the grin pulling at my cheeks, hard.

"Hey, you," I said. "What are you doing here?"

"Hey," she said. "Look outside!"

She pointed through the glass doors, and my heart sank. At first, I thought something had happened, a wreck or something outside. It was the only explanation I could come up with at first. Then it sunk in. A film crew was outside, large logos of the local news station on the microphones and on the sides of the cameras. A tall, ethnically ambiguous young woman with enough makeup on it probably added a pound of weight to her, was standing at the corner, a cameraman in front of her as they chatted.

"What?" I muttered as the realization dawned on me.

"They want to do a story on you for a segment about highlighting good in the community," she said excitedly. "Isn't that awesome?"

There was a moment of silence as I tried to process it. This had to be a joke, right?

Right?

"No," I said plainly. The levity was gone from my voice. Anger was slowly seeping in to replace it, like lava.

"What?"

I felt the anger bubbling up, but it wasn't the primary problem. It was the hurt.

"I already told you I don't want publicity for what I do here," I said. "The attention isn't why I do it or I would have already plastered my face on social media like everyone else does. I do this to do good."

"Yeah, but imagine how much good it will do if people see someone as successful as you doing this," she began.

"No," I said. "No. Absolutely not. Tell them to leave. Now."

She looked stunned, her jaw moving independently for a few moments as she tried to come up with something to say. The anger was somehow building in my chest. How dare she do this after I explicitly told her I didn't want it?

"I can't do that," she muttered. "They're already out there. They are prepared to do a story. They won't listen to me if I just tell them, 'Oops, it's over, go home.'"

"Well, I'm not going to speak to them," I said. "And I think it's awful of you to have brought a camera here to show people who are going through a really crappy time in their life and might not want to be seen on camera for the whole damn city to see."

"I..." she began, but I was on a roll now.

"Not to mention," I continued. "Some of these people are hiding from abusive spouses. Some of them from parents who hurt them, and they are over eighteen. These are *people*, Alex. Not news stories. Not characters for an Instagram post about how amazing I am for being charitable. They are *people*, with lives that can be really screwed up by being on camera. You could put them in very real danger by broadcasting where they are. Do you even realize that?"

"No," she muttered, her voice low and clearly hurt.

"Make them leave," I said. "Immediately."

With that, I turned on my heel and stomped back to the counter I had been before. The ladies had already made themselves scarce, having seen the whole thing. I watched as one of them walked up to her, presumably to get her to leave and maybe speak to some of them outside. I thought it was Essy, which would make sense, but I was too angry to look back and check.

I tried to set things up as I had been before, but I was so angry I couldn't. I stomped back down the hall, past Margaret's office and out the back door and into the sunlight, where I could fume in peace.

Chapter Twenty-One

Alexis

I felt stung and for a second, I couldn't move. It was like Nick's outburst hit me and turned me to stone. I blinked a few times, trying to process it, to come back to normal. I was stunned by his reaction, but at the same time, I knew I shouldn't have been. The voice in the back of my mind was telling me this was what I should have expected.

Because of course, it was. I had sprung this on him. Not only had I sprung it on him, but I'd actually gone directly against what he'd said and made the decision I thought was the right one, convincing myself if he just saw how well it turned out and how much good it did, he would know doing the segment was the right thing and agree with me that he should be bringing more attention to his charitable deeds.

In essence, I had done to him the same thing my family did to me. I'd ignored Nick's wishes and instead replaced them with my own understanding of the situation and my own beliefs about how it should be handled. I'd spent my entire life being angry and upset because my parents didn't listen to me. Because they dismissed my thoughts and discounted my feelings. Because they told me that what they thought was always going to be better, and I couldn't make my own decisions.

I'd spent my whole life pushing back against that, and yet somehow, I'd managed to do the same thing to Nick without batting an eye.

I felt absolutely terrible. As much as I believed he deserved to be showcased and everything he was doing should be shown off, not just because it would put on display what a fantastic guy he was and further elevate his business, but because it would bring attention to the center, it wasn't my place to make this decision. It wasn't my place to decide how Nick wanted to present himself to the public or if he wanted anyone to know about what he did for the shelter and community center. That was for him to choose, and I'd taken that choice from him. I deserved for him to be angry with me. I'd disrespected him and embarrassed him in front of people he clearly cared about.

Forcing myself to control my emotions so I could properly communicate, I went to work doing damage control. The first people I spoke with were the camera crew and producers.

"I'm so sorry," I said, walking toward them. "That obviously wasn't supposed to happen. I didn't mean for you to get that kind of footage."

"I'd hope not," one of the producers said. "So what's going on now? Are we going to get this story or not?"

"No," I said. "I'm sorry. This is my fault. You can absolutely blame me. Nick isn't interested in being a part of the feature, and I shouldn't have set this up without consulting with him first. I don't want you to think he's a bad guy or that his personality is what you just saw. That's not him. He's really amazing and spends so much time with the shelter because he really cares about people and wants to do anything he can for them. He just doesn't want that publicized. I hope you understand."

The producer nodded. "Of course, I do. It's a disappointment. This whole setup looks great, and Nick strikes me as the kind of local business owner we want people knowing about. It's the whole reason we started doing this feature. Not to mention he isn't bad to look at, and that never hurts. Now we've set ourselves up for wanting him, and we've also wasted our time now that he won't do it. We don't have anyone to fill in for him."

"I know. I'm sorry. That's my fault. I will find you someone else. Just give me a day or two, and I'll find someone to fill the gap," I said.

They were very understanding, considering the situation, and I helped them get everything back out into their vans and on their way. When they were gone, I called Nick. I needed to explain what happened and apologize. But he didn't answer. I called again and again, but it finally started going right to voicemail, and I got the hint. He was hurt, angry, and didn't want to have anything to do with me right then. And I deserved that. I gave up, knowing he needed some space. Hopefully I could give him some time to cool off and then be able to talk this through with him.

I'd be lying if I said I didn't go to bed that night hoping I would wake up to a call from Nick. But by morning, I knew it was ridiculous. This wasn't going to blow over that quickly, and I couldn't realistically hope that he would be the one to reach out to me. Even though I'd called him probably a dozen times the day before, it was still going to need to be me who bridged the gap I'd created between us.

I couldn't think about it right then. It was the day before the wedding, and I had too many things I needed to do to get ready. Gabriela was relying on me to be her maid of honor no matter how I was feeling, and I couldn't let her down. This was her time, and she deserved to have the focus on her. That meant putting a smile on my face and meeting her and the other bridesmaids at the salon for a day of pampering to prepare for the wedding. I told myself maybe a day of getting a manicure, pedicure, facial, massage, and hair treatments was just what I needed to relax and gain a better perspective about this whole situation.

But my friends knew me far too well. Even with every bit of my effort going into trying to be fully engaged with them and to enjoy this final event leading up to the big day the next day, they could tell I was distracted and upset.

We were sitting in pedicure chairs, our feet in soothing bubbling water as our hands soaked in paraffin treatments when Gabriela looked right at me.

"All right, Alex, what's going on?" she asked.

"What do you mean?" I asked, hoping I could manage to sound surprised at the question.

She gave me a look that said everything without a single word coming out of her mouth.

"You look awful," Valerie said.

We were officially at the place in our lives and the point in our friendship when there wasn't any point in tacking on the insincere and trite "no offense" people somehow thought either took the edge off what they said or released them of any responsibility of the impact.

"I'm just not wearing any makeup," I said. "I probably look more tired than usual."

"No," Gabriela said, shaking her head. "That's not it. We know what you look like without makeup on. There's something else going on. What is it?"

"I don't want to get into it. Today is about you. You're getting married tomorrow. We're here to celebrate you and make sure you have all the support and love you need. I want you to just enjoy yourself. Don't think about me," I said, trying to wave her off.

"It doesn't work like that. It doesn't matter if I'm getting married tomorrow. You're my best friend right now. And I can tell something is really bothering you. I'm not going to be able to relax and just think about myself when I'm worried about you. Just tell us what's going on," Gabriela said.

I tried to think of something else I could say that might get me out of the spotlight, but I knew that was futile. Finally, I relented.

"I did something I thought was good and that turned out to be really awful, and I think I might have ruined things with Nick," I said.

"Ruined things with Nick?" Valerie asked.

I nodded. The girls looked at each other, exchanging those kinds of knowing glances that only came from years of friendship and helping each other through countless difficult situations.

"Go on," Tracy said. "Spill."

I took a breath and let it out, then told them the whole story.

"It was stupid of me," I said as I finished. "I know it was. But I didn't think of it that way. I just thought he was being shy, and when he saw how good it could be, he would be happy he did it. Now that I've thought through it, I know it's just the same controlling nonsense my parents have put me through, and I hate that I did that to him."

"It was a mistake," Valerie said. "And it was something you thought was really positive. You were trying to give him credit for something wonderful and do something good for his future. It was misdirected, but at least you weren't doing something directly harmful."

"He saw it that way," I said. "He was really angry and really hurt. And he felt like I'd just thrown the people who were at the shelter to the wolves. That wasn't my intention at all."

"We know it wasn't," Gabriela said. "And if you give him a little time to process it, he'll know it, too." She looked at me for a second, her eyes softening. "It's obvious you really like him."

"We're friends," I said, not wanting to confirm any other feelings. "And he's been really amazing to do these things for me. Since the very beginning before he even knew me. I don't want to think I hurt him or did anything that could ruin our friendship."

"It's going to be all right. You just need to find a way to apologize."

When I got back to the building, I noticed the lights were on in the shop. He must have been there, likely finishing things for the wedding. I went up to my apartment trying to think of something that would let me reach out to him and apologize.

Chapter Twenty-Two

Nick

The wedding was the next day, and I couldn't let myself get distracted. There was just too much left to do.

The dust-up with Alex was disturbing, but at the same time, I couldn't let it completely overwhelm me. It was a mistake. Eventually, I would be over it. Or I wouldn't, and things would never be the same again. Either way, I had a commitment to fulfil, and I wasn't going to break it. My word was worth more to me than that.

Most of the desserts and snacks were in a stage of finishing that meant I barely had to do anything to them. Some needed to be frozen so they could stay as fresh as possible, others just needed a sprinkle of gold dust here, a pearl there, something to spruce it up one last time and get it ready for the big day.

Still, there were a few things that needed a bit more attention. Special truffles I was making for the guests to take home with them still needed to be made. I only had one small batch done, and I was going to need a lot more than that. Of course, the truffles could fly to the wayside if it meant I could get the big issue that needed to be finished done.

"Man, this is going to suck," I said to myself, staring at the half-finished wedding cake.

The cake was going to travel in several pieces and then be assembled on site. It meant no one would have to carry a multi-tiered cake for one, and that each piece could be touched up without having to touch up the whole thing while standing on a ladder. It was really the only way to do it, and I was still collecting the pieces I would need to pack away to finish the detailing while I was there. It was going to have to be a very early day.

Hours had gone by as I blasted music and tried to focus on my job. There was a lot of intricate detail, enough that I was actually rather proud of the job I was doing. It was going to be a crowning achievement for me, something that I hadn't really seen coming. I wasn't a wedding cake designer. I was a guy who owned a coffee shop. This was out of my wheelhouse. And yet, here I was, having done something I was proud enough that I would show Buddy Valastro.

I went to wash my hands, needing to switch from fondant to flour again, and heard a clinking sound that didn't seem to match the music. I turned around and sighed when I saw what the source was.

Alex was tapping on the glass. I caught her gaze, and she pointed to the doorhandle and mouthed for me to let her in. I watched her mime for a moment and then wiped my hands with the towel, tossing it onto the sink and heading that way.

She looked sheepish as I walked toward her, one hand behind her back and her big eyes blinking innocently. It was hard to stay mad at her, especially doing that. She looked adorable. I was still upset, but the real anger had long since gone away. It was more general disappointment and sadness now.

I unlocked the door, opening it enough for her to slip inside and then shut it behind her, locking it up. I didn't want to be bothered this evening, but I would make one lone exception. I wondered if she knew how big a deal that really was.

"First, before you say anything, I want to say I am sorry," she said, closing her eyes as she spoke, and then opening one eye experimentally when she finished the sentence before continuing. "I have an apology offering for you, and this time, I promise, I made it myself."

"You don't have a great history with that," I said.

"I know, but this time it's real. I think that won't be in doubt."

She pulled her arm out from behind her, and I laughed out loud in spite of myself.

She was presenting me with a small white paper plate, containing an overstuffed peanut butter and jelly sandwich.

"Wow," I said.

"Do you like it?" she asked, laughing as well.

"Yes," I said, taking it from her. "It's perfect. You even cut it into triangles."

"See?" she said. "Cheffing."

"Yeah," I said. "That's about the extent of it. Come on in."

I walked away, carrying the plate with me to the table where I kept my drinks and a now dried and inedible sandwich from hours earlier that I simply forgot to eat. I tossed it away and replaced the spot with the PB and J.

"Can I get you something to drink?" I asked.

"No, thank you," she said. "I'm not done apologizing. If you will just give me a minute, I have some things I have to say."

"Go ahead," I said.

I tried to prepare myself for what she was going to say. I was still hurt and angry about the whole thing, but it was hard to be close to her without the feelings coming back. I wanted to hear what she had to say, to find out if there was any way she would actually be able to explain herself. But I also didn't want to let myself be manipulated.

"I just wanted to show everyone how amazing you are," she said. "That was the entire point of the film crew. To show you off. You are incredible, Nick. Like, incredibly incredible. I wanted the whole world to know that. The world needs good guys. You are a real-life good guy. I thought it would be good for everyone if they saw you being a good guy like that. It would help your business and help the shelter and help people who needed a little brightness in the world. It would just be good for everyone."

"I appreciate that," I said. "But I told you I didn't want anyone to know about my volunteer work. I don't need to advertise what I'm doing. I don't need to make it about me. I told you that, and you still went behind my back and set that film crew up."

"I get that, but—" she began.

"No, listen to me, Alex," I said. "I want to remain anonymous. I meant that when I said it the first time. I don't do it for fame or attention, and I absolutely do not do it in any way to help my business. That's just ... ugh. It's sleazy to me. I hate when people advertise what charities they donate to, but I can get raising awareness sometimes. But not something like that. Not the shelter when there are people's lives involved."

"I understand," she said.

"I appreciate you made sure it didn't get out into the media," I said.

"I get that," she said. "But you should really take one of the outlets or culinary shows up on their offers to highlight you some day. Even if you don't mention the charities specifically, it might make people more charitable themselves in general."

"I'll think about it,' I said. "But I have to be honest, I don't see myself changing my mind. I'm not a guy that wants to see his face on TV. I just want to run a shop and have loyal, happy customers. That's all."

"I understand," she said. "So you forgive me?"

"Yes," I said through a mouthful of sandwich. "I forgive you."

Alex smiled and stepped up closer to kiss my cheek.

"Thank you."

I returned her smile and reached out to wrap my arms around her waist, pulling her a little closer. "Do you want to stay and help? I'm almost done, but I have an hour or so left."

"I can't," she said, looking disappointed. "I need to get some rest. I have to be at the hotel really early to help get everything set up and make sure Gabriela has everything she needs."

"All right. Well, I'll see you tomorrow morning, then," I said.

Alex looked up at me with softness in her big eyes that could melt me.

"You're still going to be my date?" she asked.

I chuckled and gave her a quick kiss. "Of course, I am. I couldn't walk into a wedding stag. What would everybody think?"

She laughed.

"We can't have the ladies gossiping about you."

"Goodnight," I said. "Sweet dreams."

"You get some sleep, too," she said. "I expect you to dance with me at the reception."

"I will."

She walked away and I felt my heart swell. Going back to my last tasks of the night, I felt more focused and productive. I looked forward to getting to bed just so I could get up the next morning and see her again.

Chapter Twenty-Three

Alexis

"Well, this has turned out better than I could have imagined," I said to myself as I went over my checklist for the day. It was color-coded, labeled, and stamped in several places, but it was nearly complete. All that was left was the bridesmaid activities for the morning of the wedding, making sure Nick got there with his food and to enjoy the ceremony.

I was pretty good at this.

Plus, I was up at six in the morning. Like an adult.

I had my dress laid out for me on the couch, shoes below and everything else I would need in the bathroom. I was only going to wear a pair of jeans and a T-shirt until I had to change at the venue, but everything was laid out so I wouldn't forget any of it. I had showered already and now was in the process of getting ready. An emergency touch-up makeup bag was by the clothes, and I even had my phone on the charger next to them, making sure it was charged and I wouldn't get distracted by it as I was getting ready.

Slipping on a pair of lacy red panties that I told myself was simply for my own enjoyment and not at all because I thought that things might play out that Nick would see them, I glanced at myself in the mirror. I felt pretty good about what was being reflected back at me. Maybe it was the big-ass smile distracting me, but I was enjoying it.

I went into the living room, feeling a bit exposed in the morning light wearing nothing more than a bra and thong panties, but the windows were mostly shut, and the ones with the blinds were open were facing buildings too low for anyone to be on my level and see inside. As I grabbed the phone and hit Nick's number, a part of me felt a little giddy about talking to him while wearing so little. It was stupid he couldn't see me, but it still felt naughty in an exciting way.

"Hey, you," he said when he answered the phone. "You're up early."

"Lots to do today," I said. "I just wanted to make sure you had everything you needed and ask if I could help with anything."

"No, I think I've got it all handled," he said. "Besides, you just said you have a bunch to do, right?"

"Well, yes," I said. "But your job is rather important, and I don't want to slip on my bridesmaid duties and let it fall between the cracks."

"No cracks," he said, laughing. "You're good. Go enjoy the wedding day festivities. And the wedding itself, I suppose."

I rolled my eyes. I didn't think there was much chance of actual enjoyment, beyond the sense of accomplishment and relief when it was all over, but I was going to try for my best friend. And lie my ass off if she asked.

"Okay, well, I promise I will come see you as soon as I get the chance," I said.

"I will hold you to that," he said. "I might sneak a few of the pastries aside just for you."

"Secret pastries," I said, "how special."

"You don't know the half of it," he said. "See you later."

"Bye," I said, hanging up and feeling like my cheeks hurt because I was smiling so hard.

My body felt electric. A part of me wanted to go back to my bedroom and take care of the urges that were building up and had nearly kept me from thinking straight while I was on the phone, but I checked the time and realized that for as early as I had gotten going, I was still running close to the edge. I needed to be at her apartment in a half an hour to help her start getting her hair ready.

Reluctantly putting on my dress and finishing getting ready, I kept an eye on the phone, just in case Nick sent another message or I got one from a potential Bridezilla.

Bridezilla Gabriella had a ring to it, now that I thought about it.

I headed over to her place ten minutes later to the chaos of pre-wedding preparation. Female family members, an official makeup person who apparently had worked on horror movies and this was her first wedding, all the bridesmaids and Gabriella were packed into one studio apartment, attempting to wrangle her into a state of normalcy.

"You know you don't have to be completely ready before we get to the venue," I said. "We can finish up when we are there."

"Yeah, that's what I'm doing," another voice in the room said just before an explosive wail from Gabriella quieted everyone.

"I just want to be *pretty*," she said before sobbing into her arms.

"Oh, Gabby, please, the makeup," the poor makeup girl said.

"Here we go," Gabriella's mother said. "All right, everybody, let's double time on everything!"

I sprang into action, along with several other people, and we spent the next couple of hours getting Gabby as pretty as a princess before I found a chance to sneak out to get some other things taken care of.

The venue was unlocked when I got there, due to several other helpers already being there to help finishing decorating. I jumped into the fray and helped get things put together until I heard the rest of the wedding party, and a still emotionally chaotic Gabriella, arrive. At that point, if I was going to see Nick, I needed to do it soon.

I slipped into the bathroom, checking myself in the mirror and freshening up as I could hear more and more voices fill the building.

The ceremony was scheduled for about an hour from now, and I still needed to get in my dress.

Thankfully there were so many people in the changing room that I didn't feel too bad sinking into the background to slip on my dress. Putting it over my head and letting it fall down over me before I took off my jeans, lest anyone see my hopeful panties, I finished getting ready quickly and slipped back out of the room to the sounds of Gabriella having her third glass of champagne and feeling much more relaxed about everything all of a sudden.

Nick was in the kitchen when I got there, finishing setting up trays of desserts that would go out when the ceremony was over. They looked incredible. Each one was a delicately decorated, delicious looking aberration from most wedding desserts of bland white cake and mints.

"These are incredible," I said, causing Nick to turn around and see me for the first time.

"Whoa. So are you," he said. "You look great."

"Thanks," I said, feeling the blush run up my cheeks. "Do you need any help getting these out to the reception hall?"

"No," he said, "I still have a couple helpers for an hour. They can help me. I just have to finish building the cake, but I'll do it out there."

"It's nice you had help," I said. "I would have done it if you needed."

"I know," he said, grinning in that way that made my stomach flutter. "It's all good. Everything will be together in a few minutes, and then I get to sit back and wait for people to tell me how good it all is."

I laughed.

"Well, about that," I said. "Gabby said that she would really love it if you came to the ceremony."

"Oh, really?" he asked. "Sure, I would love to. Is it all right if I'm in chef whites?"

"I'm sure she won't mind." I laughed.

"I have an extra jacket," he said. "I'll at least be clean."

"Wouldn't want to have streaks of icing on your jacket." I laughed. "No, it's fine. She just would like you to be there."

"Absolutely," he said. "Starts at one, right? Shouldn't you be down there?"

I glanced at the clock on the wall and gasped.

"Oh shit," I muttered. "Yeah, I have to go. I'll see you out there?"

"Yup," he said. "Getting the cake done and then I'll come."

"See you out there," I said, already running as fast as I dared in these heels.

I made it to the changing room just in time for the wedding coordinator to call for the bridesmaids to come get in line. Right under the wire. Thankfully, no one seemed to have noticed, everyone seemingly assuming I was taking care of something important.

Which I was.

Flirting with the caterer was extremely important.

The next half an hour was a bit of a blur. I followed the directions and tried to remember everything but lost track a few times as my mind wandered off and my eyes darted to the door until Nick came in. He came inside, almost ducking and walking quietly until he made it to the very last row of seats on the bride's side. He made eye contact with me as soon as he sat, and I smiled so widely that I almost forgot where I was.

I tried to pay attention to the ceremony as best I could. My best friend was in the process of getting married, a huge deal, and yet my eyes kept slipping back to Nick. Sitting there with a wide grin on his face and his clean, white chef's coat on, he stuck out in the crowd of black jackets and bored or sleepy expressions. He seemed to be genuinely enjoying the ceremony.

When Gabriella finally said 'I do' and walked back down the aisle with her new husband, it was my turn to walk down with one of the groomsmen. As we passed the row where Nick sat, I shot a glance his way, and he winked. I felt a flush go through me and hoped that I wasn't going to end up looking like a lobster in the pictures.

As soon as we were in the tiny little room that had been set up for photos, I found myself feeling like I was having something very close to fun. The rotating hands shoving champagne in my face probably didn't hurt. I had put a couple of them back and was feeling rather good.

The pictures finally done, we all lined up again to get introduced at the reception. As soon as the door opened, I saw Nick waiting behind the table of desserts, and he smiled so brightly I wondered if anyone else saw it. It felt so obvious. So clearly meaningful.

Unfortunately, I couldn't just go to him and spend the rest of the day hanging out. There were still responsibilities to handle. Making sure the gift table was set up, filled, emptied periodically and the gifts locked in a secure place, greeting guests, most of whom I had never spoken more than a dozen words to, and then the myriad of silly traditions and toasts that Gabriella insisted on.

By the time the cake was wheeled out, I was very ready to see Nick, and as soon as our eyes met, it was like the rest of the room faded away. I honestly worried he might drop the cake on the way with the distraction, but he calmly stopped right on his mark and embraced Gabby, shook the groom's hand, and slipped back behind them.

The cake itself was gorgeous. Exactly what Gabriella had mentioned when she talked about it, and something that I knew we never could have gotten done with anyone else. They wouldn't have put as much time and care into it as Nick obviously had.

I caught him looking at me a few times and smiled back. It wasn't long before someone noticed. Of course it had to be Gabby.

"Making eyes at the caterer, huh?" she asked, putting her fork into her cake.

"Shouldn't you be doing the doll-eyed thing with your new husband?" I asked, knowing my blush was giving me away.

"Oh, I've got the rest of my life for that," she laughed. "But I feel like if you two don't stop staring at each other, I might need to ask the minister to stick around for another ceremony."

"Hush," I said. "Eat your cake. Enjoy your wedding."

"Oh, I am," she said, grinning. "If I had a guess, I will enjoy the wedding night only marginally more than you will."

"Gabriella!" I said, but she was already turning away, cackling as she headed back to her new groom.

The truth was, I felt like I was getting ahead of myself. I didn't know what was going on between us, especially after the fight. But whatever was going on, I didn't want to jinx it. It felt pretty damn good. And I was placing bets with myself on how likely it was that someone else was going to see the lace under all this fabric.

Chapter Twenty-Four

Nick

Things were going pretty well, I thought.

The cake was exactly what I was hoping it would turn out to be, and the bride seemed to love it. Everyone else was clearly enjoying the desserts, and I had been approached on a couple of occasions about the possibility of doing another event. Considering this was the first large-scale event I had ever done, I thought that was a good sign, even if I was mostly telling people I wasn't really set up for that kind of thing.

A dozen business cards and a couple of handwritten phone numbers scratched onto napkins gave me the idea that maybe I should. Granted, a few of those phone numbers I felt might have an ulterior motive.

But my favorite part of the entire night, even above watching people really enjoy the food I prepared or marvel at the designs or the cake, is the little sneaking glances at Alex that I had been stealing the entire wedding and reception. Seeing her send back little smiles every time she caught my eye made my stomach clench.

I was standing by the dessert table, making sure everything was full when I saw her breaking away from the gaggle of bridesmaids and heading toward me. I stepped around the tables to greet her and had to smile back at the beaming expression on her slightly sweaty face.

"Hey, I finally got a few minutes," she said. "I think, actually, I might be done. But who knows?"

"Awesome," I said.

"Is there anything I can help you with?"

"Hell, no," I laughed. "You've been running around doing enough. As a matter of fact, I think you need this."

I handed her a glass of champagne and laughed as she threw it back like a shot.

"Yes, that was absolutely what I needed," she said. "Maybe like eighteen more."

"Well, perhaps not that," I said. "However, I was wondering if you would like to go dance."

"Yes." She said it with such an emphatic voice that it got another laugh out of me. "Come on, the music is great!"

She reached out her hand, and I took it, grinning all the way to the dance floor.

The sexual tension was immediate as soon as we got into the crowd of strangers. The other bridesmaids were elsewhere, still dealing with responsibilities and duties while Alex and I began to dance. It didn't matter if they had something else for her, I was pretty sure she wasn't leaving the dance floor. Nor would I have let her.

My hand slid over her waist as we got closer and closer, and soon her breath was on my neck, and I felt myself getting closer to her lips. Soon, our noses touched, and we were drawn together like magnets. Our lips touched, and when we separated we were both grinning like lunatics. Another kiss followed and another, and soon we were laughing, dancing harder than ever and caught up completely in the moment.

After a few songs, we were both out of breath.

"All right," she said. "I haven't had any of these treats yet, and it looks like the table is emptying out. I have to try some."

"Well, come on then." I laughed, taking her hand and leading her away from the mass of people still dancing.

I led her to the table and immediately pointed out two of the desserts I was most excited about.

"Try this," I said, handing her a pastry with orange zest that I had eaten a few of while making.

"Oh, dame, this is good," she said, moaning. "No wonder there's only like four of them left."

"Right?" I said. "Granted, part of that is because I didn't have as many when I got here as the others because I ate a few on my own."

She laughed. "They're really good. What else?"

"Oh, try these," I said, handing her another one. I grabbed us both a glass of champagne, and we went across the table and shared a few of them.

It was beginning to feel like I wasn't there as a caterer. I was a guest. Specifically Alex's guest. Her date.

It was an incredible feeling. I felt like I was walking on clouds as we drank and ate and laughed. The festivities continued around us, and it didn't matter. The whole world could burn down, and I wouldn't care. Not as long as I got to extend this time with her, right now.

"So that over there is Rain Founders," she said, pointing out an angular-looking man with his belt tied really far up his waist.

"Oh, tell me about Rain Founders," I said.

"Okay, so, he looks like an accountant who might have been born on Mars, but he is actually a former prizefighter," she said.

I laughed. "No way," I said. "No way that's true."

"It isn't." She laughed. "I actually have no idea who that is. Oh! That guy over there—" She pointed to a portly man who had a plate of my pastries in front of him as he sat at one of the round tables. "I know him!"

"Give it to me," I said. "Who is he?"

"Former professional bowler Frank Sammartino," she said. "He's Tammy's father."

"Oh," I said, pretending I remembered which person she had previously pointed out as Tammy.

"He was on TV a bunch during the nineties. Won a bunch of tournaments. He wears these rings he won all the time. You can see one of them shining on his right hand, see it?"

"Wow, that is one hell of a ring," I laughed.

She continued to point out various other people, telling me stories about them or about how her life had been before she met me. I felt like I was starting to really get to know her. The real her. Not just the girl I'd flirted with and had come to an arrangement with, but the person she had grown to be.

It was intoxicating.

There was a joy that emanated from her, and I wanted to drink it in. She was happy, in an element that she enjoyed, and had worked hard to make sure it went perfectly and succeeded. Clearly, the connection between us had gotten stronger, more intense, and it only added to the elation of the moment. I didn't want it to end.

"I think," she said, putting her plate down and turning to look at me, "as much as I absolutely adore your food, that I have had enough sweets."

"Oh, me too," I said. "I don't think I can eat any more sugar."

"And yet," she said, "I'm hungry."

"Working all day will do that to you," I said. "Me too, actually. The more I think about it, I feel like I could really, really go for something that isn't tiny and themed. Like..."

"Pizza. Tacos. Buffalo chicken," she said, rattling them off with a dreamy look in her eye.

"Yes," I said. "To all of them. If I could make a taco out of buffalo chicken pizza, that would be ideal."

She laughed.

"I don't know if that sounds terrible or amazing, but I am game to find out."

A swell of music seemed to fill the entire place, and we both looked back toward the table where the cake was sitting. A crowd of people, including two photographers, were descending on it.

"They're going to cut the cake," she said excitedly, grabbing my hand. "Come on."

We made our way across the room until we were near the collection of people including the bride and groom. There were flashes from the cameras going off constantly as she sliced a giant portion out and fed it to her now-husband to the cheers of the crowd, including Alex and myself.

"I'm so glad they didn't do the whole shoving it in the face thing," she said as the bride and groom walked away and I led her to the area behind them. "I hate that. Hey, where are we going?"

"Over here," I said. "I have to divvy out the slices of the cake for people."

"I can help," she said, beaming, and I grinned.

We took the plates assigned for the cake pieces, and I began slicing out even portions, placing them on the plates that Alex was holding and then handing them out to guests. When the line of guests had finally finished, I sliced another and put it on a plate for Alex and then one for myself.

"Finally our turn?" she asked.

"As long as you don't mind something else sweet," I said.

"I think I can handle one more thing," she said.

We tucked ourselves away, just off to the side of the room while we dug into our cake slices. It was nice being somewhere a bit quieter, a bit less busy. Private. As private as we could get here, at least. Watching her stick her fork into the cake and place it between her deep red lips was a dessert of her own, but it was made better by the closing of her eyes and smile that crossed her face immediately after.

"Like it?" I asked.

"It is—and I am being completely honest—the best wedding cake I've ever had," she said. "Normally they are so bland."

"I know," I said. "I was determined not to let that happen here."

I took a forkful of the cake into my own mouth and nodded. I had to say, it was pretty damn good.

Chapter Twenty-Five

Alexis

"No," I said, waving off the third straight person who came to compliment Nick and ended up complimenting me as well at Nick's insistence. "I cannot take credit. As I keep saying. I barely did anything."

"Not true," he said. "I couldn't have done it without her help."

"He's lying," I laughed.

The gentleman who was standing in front of us laughed as well, looking between us with a knowing smile.

"Well, whoever is responsible for the desserts and the cake did a marvelous job," he said. "And you two make a fabulous couple."

"I..." I began and stopped as he winked and turned away. "Thank you!"

Nick glanced over at me with an eyebrow cocked. I pushed his leg and took another big sip of my champagne.

It had been fun seeing him basking in all the compliments and generally spending time with him. After the hecticness of the wedding itself, it was nice to let loose a little and just enjoy myself but doing it with Nick by my side was a whole other level. Sharing that joy, that sense of accomplishment, it was astonishing how good it felt.

My feelings were getting stronger, and it was becoming an issue of wanting to get to spend more time with him alone. I didn't want to share him anymore, as much fun as I was having at the wedding. I wanted him alone. Or at least just somewhere that people wouldn't interrupt us. Even just a quiet night at a park or restaurant or something. Anywhere I could just be in a tiny little world with him.

"Nick?" another voice said in front of me, and I looked up. It was another person I vaguely recognized through the festivities but still had no clue as to who it was.

"Hi," Nick said, smiling.

"I'm Amanda," she said, as if that narrowed things down.

"Hi Amanda," Nick said, taking this with far less questions than I was. "Nice to meet you."

"Nice to meet you," she said, and something inside me wasn't terribly pleased by the way her eyes seemed to be stuck on him and not acknowledging my existence. "I just wanted to say that these little pastries, they are my favorite. Some of the best desserts I've ever had."

"Oh, wow, thank you," he said with the same genuine expression of humble gratefulness he had expressed multiple times tonight. It was adorable, and frankly attractive. He seemed to really be touched by every person that liked his food.

"I just couldn't get enough of the pastries," she continued, "or the macarons. Oh my..." She moaned and licked her lips, "the macarons."

"Oh, yeah, I love those too. Alex helped a lot with those."

He turned toward me with his honest, slightly glassy-eyed expression.

"I helped," I said, happy to get her attention off him for a second, but still not wanting to take credit, "but only a little. Nick is the one that's responsible for all this."

Amanda nodded, seeming to be not retaining a word I was saying, but waiting politely for me to be finished so she could direct her attention back to Nick. As soon as the words were out of my mouth, she turned back to him.

"I would love to get your recipe sometime," she said.

"Oh, I don't give out recipes," he said. "Sorry."

"Speaking of recipes," I said, getting his attention and feeling a bit of relief when the woman turned, pouting a bit, and walked away, "I have a recipe for the rest of the evening. It involves being at my place in pajamas. Maybe watching a movie. Would you like to come and hang out with me? Maybe even order a pizza?"

He laughed.

"You know, ever since we mentioned eating real food, my mind has been drifting over to pizza," he said. "I would love that."

There was a warmth in his eyes that told me it wasn't just about the food. He was feeling what I was feeling. Neither one of us wanted the night to end. Not yet. Maybe not for a while. The kisses we had stolen all night, spiriting away for them in corners or while dancing on the dance floor, had certainly told me that he was feeling the same way I was.

"Well, I need to go get my stuff from the bridal room," I said. "Also, make sure the gifts and cards and stuff have been sent to the honeymoon suite. It should only take a few minutes."

"Okay," he said. "I can hang out here until you are done. I have some of my people coming in to do clean-up of my stuff, so I can go whenever."

"Oh?"

"Yeah," he said. "They offered to do it for free, just to help out, but I'm going to pay them anyway. They just don't know yet."

He put his finger over his mouth, indicating the secret.

I tapped my own lips with my forefinger.

"I won't say a word," I said. "So you wait here. I'll be back in a couple minutes. It seriously shouldn't take long."

"Sounds good," he said.

As I walked away, my eyes scanned the room and found Amanda, currently hanging on some other guy on the dance floor. It wasn't like I was jealous. I just didn't want her near Nick. That wasn't the same thing. Right?

Not that I thought it would matter. Nick was giving me the same vibes I felt like I was giving off. And if I was right, tonight could be something really special.

I headed out to do what I needed to do, starting with grabbing my things from the bridal room. No one else was in there to slow me down, although I did note that several pieces of clothing had been discarded here, and at least one bridesmaid dress had been removed and theoretically replaced by a backup. Either that or we had a naked bridesmaid somewhere, which while not likely, I had to admit wasn't impossible.

The gifts and cards were supposed to be all in one room, and when I went to check on it, I noticed one of the nephews of the groom standing by the door.

"Are you in charge of gift security?" I asked the pimply-faced, gangly teen.

"Yes, ma'am," he said.

Oof. I didn't like having to get used to that.

"Good," I said. "I am in charge of making sure they get to the honeymoon suite. Are they ready to go?"

"Sure," he said. "Do you need any help?"

I looked back down the long hall, into the main room where I could still see Nick sitting at the table, now talking to one of the other men I didn't recognize. I wanted to get back to him. Or rather, I wanted him and me to be somewhere else. Preferably with food on our stomachs. Stomachs that had less layers of clothing on them.

"Yes," I said. "That would be great. If you could just help me get them up to the room, that would be amazing."

"Sure," he said.

With all the vocabulary variety of the average teenage boy, he went into the room with me, helping me gather everything and then placing it on a cart. We started for the door and headed out to get them to their final destination.

Ten minutes later, everything was put away, the young man relieved of his duties so he could go enjoy the desserts and be nervous around girls, and I was on my way back to Nick. As I rounded a corner that headed past the restrooms and to the main floor, I nearly ran headlong into Mr. Goldman, one of my father's business associates. I had known him almost all my life and had spoken to him earlier in the night.

"Hey again," he said, waving.

I waved back, hoping to bypass him on his way to the restroom as I headed to Nick. Mr. Goldman could be a talker, and I didn't feel like getting caught up in a conversation at the moment. Unfortunately, that was precisely what was on his mind.

"Before I miss out on talking to you again before you leave," he said, "I wanted to get your opinion on something."

"Sure," I said, resigning myself to at least a couple of minutes of his time. Hopefully his bladder wouldn't allow it to be too long.

"I've been interested in doing some investing and maybe spreading out to some other locations. Perhaps even franchising the business."

"Oh?" I asked. "I thought you liked being the only say. Dad tried to talk you into franchising years ago."

"I know, I know, and I was an old fool to say no then," he laughed. "But here's the thing. I've been thinking about it a lot recently, and tonight I came here and had one of Nick's baked goods. It blew me away. And I saw you've been sitting with him. Rather closely too, I might add."

His massive, wild eyebrows waggled, and I laughed. He waved me to follow him back away from the entrance to the main room and closer to where the bathrooms were around the corner.

"Yes, we are very close," I admitted.

"Well, then you might be able to help me out then," he said. "I was thinking I might be able to get some of Nick's baked goods packaged and sold online, or perhaps in stores. If I franchised out, I don't see why I couldn't put him in my stores."

"Oh, wow," I said.

"I think, if he was willing, we could really expand his business by leaps and bounds. There is a lot of potential there for growth, and I think that with the right infrastructure and the right minds behind it, his business could be huge, much bigger than one storefront." He grinned and did that thing old men do where they pull their chin down to look at you over the rims of their glasses and dropping their voice a little, as if what they are saying is sage advice that simply should not be ignored. "Something like this, if you had your hand in it, would be awfully good on a resume as well, don't you think?"

"I think you might be right," I said, glancing down at my phone and seeing how long I had been gone. I just wanted to get past him and back to the table. But at the same time, he was making a lot of sense. "I think that would be awfully good for my career, for sure."

"The key is," he said, "getting in on the ground floor. Being among the first. I just want to make sure no one beats me to the punch."

"Of course," I said. "That makes perfect sense."

Chapter Twenty-Six

Nick

The guy I was talking to seemed to know who I was despite me not having a clue who he was. It didn't really bother me. He seemed like a nice guy who might be a fun person to be around when sober, but at the moment, he was one or two drinks away from taking a nap and was slurring a lot as we discussed the finer points of steak.

How we got on to the subject of steak was still a mystery. Much like how, when, and why the entire conversation began in the first place. It was as if I showed up mid-conversation and was just expected to keep up. Only I hadn't moved from my chair. He brought the conversation, already in progress, to me.

"And then I... then I..." He hiccupped and shook his head. "And then I make sure to put it onto the plate *hot*."

"Oh," I said, trying to be polite.

"None of that resting stuff," he said, the last two words barreling into each other like people standing in a tight line.

"No resting, huh?" I asked, looking around for Alex. She had been gone a long time. Or maybe just being around this gentleman made ten minutes seem an awful lot more like a half an hour.

"Nope," he said, popping the letter 'p' comically. "It's a waste of time, and I like to eat my steak hot."

"Wow," I said, feigning as much interest as I could.

"S'cuse me," he said suddenly. "My wife is over on the dance floor. I need to get my boogie on."

"Boogie away, my friend," I said.

"I will," he said, rather emphatically. "Boogie down!"

As he trudged away, as mysteriously as he came, I slid out of my own chair and started making my way toward the hall I'd seen Alex disappear down. I wanted to tell her I was going to get the van ready and put some of the stuff in there that I knew needed to go in a certain way before the rest of it got packed by my helpers. Then I could head back to the shop with them and unpack, and they could do the cleaning while I headed out with Alex.

I was feeling really optimistic and light on my feet as I made my way across the floor. This had turned into a fantastic day. And now that I had a couple glasses of water in me, I was able to tell that it wasn't the alcohol that was making me feel this way either. It was feeling really *real*.

This could be the beginning of something amazing.

I went into the hall, looking in a couple of directions for her. The bridal room was just a few doors down, but it was seemingly empty. The room just another door down from that and across the hall was open, and it looked like it had been the gift room. It too was empty. Which meant Alex was either on her way back or already here. I just had to find her.

I went back out onto the floor and was bombarded by a few more people who wanted to talk about the cake and the desserts and get my information. Thankfully, I had a stack of business cards in my pocket and was able to hand them out, directing them to where the shop was while simultaneously asking if anyone had seen Alex. A couple people said they had talked to her, but no one was sure where she was now.

Walking the perimeter of the room, I happened to look down a different hallway and saw Alex talking with an older gentleman I recognized as one of her father's business associates. Just as I saw them, he motioned for her to follow him as they talked, and they disappeared around a corner.

I crossed the room, pretending not to hear the shout of my inebriated steak connoisseur friend as he hollered toward me, and tried to follow them. As I got close to the corner, I could hear their voices. And what they were saying.

They were talking about me. And my business. And the man was making it very clear he was interested in starting a few franchises of The Coffee Shop and wanted to get in on the ground floor. I stopped, eavesdropping on the conversation from around the corner as he tried to get information from Alex.

"Yeah, I've seen his books," she said, making my stomach drop and my heart race. "The financial success of his business is incredible. I mean really, the potential is there for his company to expand rapidly. I'm sure he will be doing that soon, if he wants. He's got everything all ready to do it, and I am sure, positive even, that the second he does, you will hear about it."

The man laughed, one of those businessman laughs that never sounds genuine. I hated it.

"I bet I will," he said. "Nothing gets past me, you know. Your father and I have done business for over thirty years. It's good to see his talents run in the family."

I had heard enough.

I turned on my heel, walking away hurt. Not just hurt. Betrayed. Furious. How dare she say something like that? Had she just used our relationship to get close to me just so she could 'get in on the ground floor'? What kind of person goes behind someone's back like that to talk about expanding a business? It was just ridiculous.

Crossing the shortest part of the main room, I made a beeline for the kitchen. My two helpers were there, and I had them help me pack things up but then sent them home. There was no need to keep them around now. I handed them both a stack of cash I had pulled aside for them, that I was going to give them later, and gave it to them anyway. As they left, I began putting things in the van, stacking it up and preparing to leave.

I happened to catch a glance at Alex, wandering through the main room, apparently looking for me. I was just fast enough at packing that she didn't see me and never made it to the kitchen to look before I was gone. There was nothing I needed to say to her right now. Nothing I wanted, either. I just wanted to get back to the shop, clean everything and put it away, and not be bothered.

This wasn't some misunderstanding or me mishearing her. This was her way overstepping her boundaries and speaking on my behalf about something she knew I didn't want to explore. At least right now. I couldn't tolerate that. I felt manipulated and taken advantage of. But worse, I was hurt and disappointed. Of all the people to do this, I never expected Alex.

When everything was in the van, I didn't hesitate to leave. There was no one in there I needed to say goodbye to. Not anymore.

I drove straight to the shop, parking on the street to bring everything in the front doors. Once it was all unloaded, I locked up the shop and started the big sink with hot water and soap.

Often, I found a good way of thinking through something that was bothering me was by taking something that needed a deep clean and going to town on it. Refrigerators, stoves, you name it, I had taken it upon myself to get them absolutely gleaming while I was working out something difficult in my head. These tools and dishes provided a perfect excuse to do just that.

As I washed the dishes, finding myself scrubbing them perhaps just a *little* too hard, I tried to take my mind off Alex. It was going to be hard. Tonight was a lot, and I had been so hopeful it was leading to something. Something that could have been so special. Right now, I was supposed to be ordering a pizza, wearing sweatpants, and curled up on a couch with Alex watching a movie or TV.

Perhaps we wouldn't even have made it to the pizza before things had been taken to another level. Or so I had thought. But now, all that was out the window.

How could I trust someone who would just blatantly speak for me like that? Especially when she was not only speaking for me, but speaking out of turn. I didn't want to franchise. I'd made that so very clear. And here she was, basically offering access to me before anyone else and forcing my hand at expanding.

Eventually, I ran out of things to clean and checked the clock. It was getting late, but I wasn't tired yet. Deciding to use my time wisely, I went about making a few things for tomorrow. Putting extreme frustration and furious anger into tiny delicate details on cupcakes was something that was difficult to do, but I managed it for a little while.

Finally having enough an hour or so later, I put everything I had made away and cleaned up my station before heading for the door. When I locked it up, I knew I would have to be back in just a few short hours, but I needed to try and get some sleep.

The thing was, no matter how disappointed I was, no matter how angry I was, I couldn't just give up on life and hide away in my room. I needed to get this shop open tomorrow and serve coffee and pastries with a smile and the same good-natured rapport that people had come to expect from me. I needed to be me.

I needed to just move forward. If that meant forgetting Alex altogether, striking it up as a meeting of two people who didn't work out but maybe the contacts I made during our time together would make it worthwhile, then that was what I was going to look at it like. The hard part was just forgetting Alex.

When I got home, I realized I was still hungry. I had been depending on that pizza.

Angry at myself and grumbling because I was tired as well, I ended up making a sandwich and eating it over the sink. As soon as I had forced it and a beer down my throat, I washed the plate, put it away and made for the shower. It wasn't going to be a long one. Just long enough to wash the day off me and get in bed. Tomorrow was going to be a long day, and I was going to have to have enough energy to face it.

Chapter Twenty-Seven

Alexis

"Anyway," I said, looking back out into the main room. I could have sworn I saw him a second ago...

"Yes, well, I am sure you will keep me abreast of anything should it change," he said, a confidence in his voice that frankly annoyed me.

"Excuse me?" I asked.

"You'll let me know when he is going to make his move," he said. "Maybe supply me with some of those raw numbers you saw. What is his overhead in that place he has, anyway? I couldn't imagine it would be much, since he doesn't have many employees. But the quality of the ingredients he is buying has to be pricier than normal. Something that might be compromised when franchising..."

"I'm sorry," I said, "I am not going to be giving out any inside information. I think perhaps I've said too much already."

He laughed, one of those big, booming businessmen laughs I heard my father do all the time. There was no humor in it.

"Your father and I have been doing business for thirty years," he said, for the third time in our conversation. "Surely, you won't begrudge me a bit of a leg up here."

"Your relationship with my father has nothing to do with me and my relationship with Nick, actually," I said. "And if I might be honest, I am kind of offended you would think it does. I am not under any obligation to tell you anything."

"You know," he said, straightening up and the smile sliding to a more menacing grin, "you could make something of yourself if you learned to use situations to your benefit."

"You mean taking advantage of someone?" I asked.

"Heh," he said, caught off guard by my response. I got the impression people didn't talk back much to him. Especially women. "You know, I've looked into Nick's background. I know where he comes from. Nothing. He comes from absolutely nothing. Someone like that, they are stupid with money, Alexis. They are easily led and easily removed from their cash. You know this. He should be easy to get to agree to do what we want."

"What *we* want?" I asked.

"Of course," he said. "You would be in line for quite a cut if we can get the deal to go through."

I felt like punching him. It was so degrading, so humiliating how he was talking to me. He was trying to manipulate me into manipulating Nick, using the same tactics he was implying I should use on him because of some perceived weakness. But on top of all that, I was also insulted on Nick's behalf.

"This conversation has run its course, I think," I said. "Nick is a smart man. And an honorable one. When he says he doesn't feel like he wants to expand, it's not him playing hard to get or angling for something. He means he doesn't want to expand. And while I think he might be making a mistake in that regard, it's *not my decision.* He knows his business, and ultimately, he runs it to keep himself happy. Something that I am sure getting into business with you would not happen."

"He would be very wealthy," he said. "Not as wealthy as me, of course, but wealthy."

I was so angry I could barely see straight. The smug smirk on his face was driving me insane, and I felt like I just needed to get out of there.

"I need you to understand something," I said. "I am not going to use Nick, and anything that happens with his business, expanding or not expanding, is up to him. And him alone. He will do with it what he wants, and right now, he doesn't want to do anything. He might not have grown up wealthy, owning chains and acting like a glorified land-lord, but that means nothing. He's smart, obviously an incredible businessman, and too damn good to be getting tangled up with sleazy businessmen who would take his ideas and modify them until they were unrecognizable.

"Now if you will excuse me, I need to go."

I didn't wait to hear a response, but I was sure there wouldn't be one. Not a rational one at least. The kind of guy he was, or had revealed himself to be, was the type who would be so angry at having their ego hit that they would immediately attack something like my looks. It was always their way.

Instead, I stomped back into the main room, looking for Nick as I occasionally found someone to say goodbye to. He wasn't where he had been, and the man who had been speaking to him didn't know where he was either. Eventually, I came across one of the waiters who said he'd seen him packing up to leave with the helpers from his shop, and I felt relieved. That meant he was getting ready to go.

All I had to do was meet him outside.

I hurried around, saying goodbye to everyone else I wanted to, and then slipped into the kitchen. The service entrance was just through one of the doors there, and when I opened it, I expected to see the bay door open and Nick standing there, loading things into his van.

Instead, the bay door was shut, and it was dark and quiet inside.

I crossed over to the little door leading outside and popped my head outside of it. My heart sank. His car wasn't there. He wasn't just loading his stuff into the van.

He had left.

I dug through the bag that had my backup dress and other things I'd left in the bridal room and found my phone. No messages or calls had been missed. Hurt confusion was starting to bubble up in my chest as I called his number, and it was amplified when he didn't answer. I waited for a few minutes, hoping he would call me back, and when he didn't, I held my thumb over the call button to call him. Just at that moment, a text came in. I opened it.

I went home. I'm going to bed.

That was it. The whole message, just seven words. Seven words and he'd left me standing at the wedding, all by myself.

Angry, confused, and hurt, I made my way back through the venue all the way to the other side where my car was parked. As I got in, I felt the tears at the corners of my eyes and fought them back. There would be time for tears in the morning. When I talked to him.

In person.

The next morning came after a fitful night's sleep, and I got myself as dressed as I felt I could manage. My hair pulled back tight and all-black-everything seemed to be the look I was going for today. Like a stagehand, wandering off into real life.

I went down to the shop and saw him, standing like usual behind the counter. He saw me too. As soon as he did, his jaw set, and he walked away from the counter to head to the back. I slipped inside and followed him.

"Where the hell did you go?" I asked as I cornered him by the big sink where a couple of the recognizable tools had yesterday were still drying.

"I figured I didn't need to tell you," he said. "Judging by the conversation I heard you having last night, you know more about my life and my business than I do. You must have already known what I was thinking."

"What?" I asked, completely confused. "What the hell are you talking about? I don't understand."

"I heard you talking to that guy about seeing my books. About how I was going to franchise soon."

His voice had risen enough that I was pretty sure everyone in the shop heard him. It was a righteous anger, furious but kept in check. He wasn't the type of guy to yell and scream. But when he was angry, you sure as hell knew it. And I sure as hell knew it right then.

"Nick, I..." I began.

"No, stop," he said. "You manipulated and betrayed me. So you can save your apologies, all right? I told you specifically that I hadn't made any decisions about expanding yet, and that I was leaning very much toward *not* franchising. I said that to you. I know you heard it. And you looking at my books wasn't something you should be discussing with other people, especially people who are outright strangers to me. It's my business."

"Nick," I tried again, but he was on a roll now.

"You had no right," he continued. "You had no right to talk about my finances or my business with anyone else."

I let like my heart was being squeezed in a vise. I couldn't get words out of my mouth, and my tongue was dry. He was so angry, and I could feel it coming off him like a fever. He didn't want anything to do with me anymore. That was clear. But I needed to try.

"Nick, can we talk? Please?"

"No," he said flatly. "I'm very busy. If you could possibly leave the shop, I can get to work on things that are extremely important for my *one* shop."

"Okay," I said, my voice very small now. It was hard to get the words out.

"Just one thing," he said, stopping me before I turned to walk through the door. "I didn't do the wedding for the business. I did it for you. For you, Alex. I wanted to help you. I liked you, and I thought you liked me too. I didn't realize this whole thing was just a plan to get what you wanted out of me. I should have realized that when the camera crew showed up at the shelter. I should have gotten it through my thick skull then, but I didn't. I gave you another chance. And then look what I get for it."

"Nick, it's not like that," I began. "This was an entirely different situation. You must not have heard the whole conversation, because..."

"Just go," he said. "I need to get back to work. I can't do that if I am standing around all afternoon with sleep deprivation and arguing with you."

"Fine," I said. "I'll leave you alone now."

Sadly, I turned, not wanting to let him see the tears stream down my face. If I could just make it to the door, that would be better. As I walked out of the shop, I thought I might have a handle on it, but a few steps later, as I pushed the button on the elevator floor, I realized I didn't.

And I wouldn't.

For a long time.

THE END

A BITTER FLAVOR
LEXY TIMMS
A BITTER FLAVOR
LEXY TIMMS
GET IT ON
Google Play
R kobo
Available at
amazon
nook
Lexy Timms

The Coffee Shop Romance

A Rich After Taste
A Bitter Flavor
Baked to Perfection

Dead Ahead FREE COPY

Tri:

I'm a Navy SEAL on a mission to find out what's happening in a politically-charged environment. When things go horribly wrong, I find myself saddled with my exact opposite: a female scientist who never runs out of questions or words. Now we're stuck on a deserted island with no way off and information vital to avoiding World War III. Will we make it off the island in time to warn the world what's coming? And will we do it with our hearts still intact?

Ashley:

They sent me to an island to find out why the marine life off the coast was behaving strangely. The only problem? It's a contested land inhabited by terrorists. When I find myself stranded on the island with a Navy SEAL who saved my life, I don't know whether we'll make it off alive. But one thing I do know? I might be falling for the man with the haunting blue eyes. Before we find out whether we have a future together, we have to escape terrorists, get off the island, and save the world.

GET YOUR <u>FREE</u> COPY BY SIGNING UP FOR AUTUMN GAZE's NEWSLETTER!!!

Autumn Gaze Newsletter:
https://www.autumngaze.com/sign-up

Find Lexy Timms:

Lexy Timms Newsletter:
http://www.lexytimms.com/newsletter
Lexy Timms Facebook Page:
https://www.facebook.com/LexyTimmsAuthor
Lexy Timms Website:
http://www.lexytimms.com

Lexy Timms
BOSS Book 3
BOSS Book 2
BOSS Book 1
Managing the BOSSES Book 1-3
Lexy Timms
FREE
for a
Limited
Time

WANT

FREE READS?

Sign up for Lexy Timms' newsletter
And she'll send you updates on new releases,
ARC copies of books and a whole lotta fun!
Sign up for news and updates!
http://www.lexytimms.com/newsletter

More by Lexy Timms:

Jamie Connors has given up on men. Despite being smart, pretty, and just slightly overweight, she's a magnet for the kind of guys that don't stay around.

Her sister's wedding is at the foreground of the family's attention. Jamie would be fine with it if her sister wasn't pressuring her to lose weight so she'll fit in the maid of honor dress, her mother would get off her case and her ex-boyfriend wasn't about to become her brother-in-law.

Determined to step out on her own, she accepts a PA position from billionaire Alex Reid. The job includes an apartment on his property and gets her out of living in her parent's basement.

Jamie must balance her life and somehow figure out how to manage her billionaire boss, without falling in love with him.

Sometimes the heart needs a different kind of saving... find out if Charity Thompson will find a way of saving forever in this hospital setting Best-Selling Romance by Lexy Timms

Charity Thompson wants to save the world, one hospital at a time. Instead of finishing med school to become a doctor, she chooses a different path and raises money for hospitals – new wings, equipment, whatever they need. Except there is one hospital she would be happy to never set foot in again—her fathers. So of course, he hires her to create a gala for his sixty-fifth birthday. Charity can't say no. Now she is working in the one place she doesn't want to be. Except she's attracted to Dr. Elijah Bennet, the handsome heartbreaker chief.

Will she ever prove to her father that's she's more than a med school dropout? Or will her attraction to Elijah keep her from repairing the one thing she desperately wants to fix?

Emily Rose Dougherty is a good Catholic girl from mythical Walkerville, CT. She had somehow managed to get herself into a heap trouble with the law, all because an ex-boyfriend has decided to make things difficult.

Luke "Spade" Wade owns a Motorcycle repair shop and is the Road Captain for Hades' Spawn MC. He's shocked when he reads in the paper that his old high school flame has been arrested. She's always been the one he couldn't forget.

Will destiny let them find each other again? Or what happens in the past, best left for the history books?

** *This is book 1 of the Hades' Spawn MC Series. All your questions may not be answered in the first book.*

Don't miss out!

Visit the website below and you can sign up to receive emails whenever Lexy Timms publishes a new book. There's no charge and no obligation.

https://books2read.com/r/B-A-NNL-MQVAC

BOOKS 2 READ

Connecting independent readers to independent writers.

Did you love *A Rich Aftertaste*? Then you should read *Surging Tide*[1] by Lexy Timms!

Sometimes, one must go against the tide...

Gabriella – Gabby for short – desperately needs a holiday. She's worked way too hard, just lost her father and wants a break. From everything. She books a stay at a picturesque cottage by the sea. No phone, no internet, no neighbors – just books, a bottle of wine and the beach. A month without distraction and a chance to find herself again.

Until a hunk of a guy suddenly shows up catching her sunbathing in her birthday suit. The man is hot as sin. Jake Wolfe is cocky and stubborn too.

Double booked. Double trouble.

---

1. https://books2read.com/u/3LyV1e

2. https://books2read.com/u/3LyV1e

Stuck on an island with a stranger, they try to make the best of it, but get on each other's nerves. When a drunken night leads to steamy passion, they realize something's brewing, and like the unpredictability of stormy weather, things could get rough

Cottage by the Sea Series

Surging TideDistant ShoresTwisting Ocean

Read more at www.lexytimms.com.

Also by Lexy Timms

12 Days of Christmas
Snowflake Hollow - Part 1
Snowflake Hollow - Part 2
Snowflake Hollow - Part 3
Snowflake Hollow - Part 4
Snowflake Hollow - Part 5
Snowflake Hollow - Part 6
Snowflake Hollow - Part 7
Snowflake Hollow - Part 8
Snowflake Hollow - Part 9
Snowflake Hollow - Part 10
Snowflake Hollow - Part 11
Snowflake Hollow - Part 12
Snowflake Hollow - Complete Series

A Bad Boy Bullied Romance
I Hate You
I Hate You A Little Bit
I Hate You A Little Bit More

A Bump in the Road Series
Expecting Love
Selfless Act
Doctor's Orders

A Burning Love Series
Spark of Passion
Flame of Desire
Blaze of Ecstasy

A Chance at Forever Series
Forever Perfect
Forever Desired
Forever Together

A Dark Casino Romance Series
High Roller
Place Your Bet
All Or Nothing

A Dark Mafia Romance Series
Taken By The Mob Boss
Truce With The Mob Boss
Taking Over the Mob Boss

Trouble For The Mob Boss
Tailored By The Mob Boss
Tricking the Mob Boss

A Dating App Series
I've Been Matched
You've Been Matched
We've Been Matched

A "Kind of" Billionaire
Taking a Risk
Safety in Numbers
Pretend You're Mine

A Maybe Series
Maybe I Should
Maybe I Shouldn't
Maybe I Did

A Royal Affair Series
Royally F*cked
Royally Screwed
Royally Obsessed

Assisting the Boss Series

Billion Reasons
Duke of Delegation
Late Night Meetings
Delegating Love
Suitors and Admirers

BBW Romance Series
Capturing Her Beauty
Pursuing Her Dreams
Tracing Her Curves

Beating the Biker Series
Making Her His
Making the Break
Making of Them

Betrayal at the Bay Series
Devil's Bay
Devil's Deceit
Devil's Duplicity

Billionaire Banker Series
Banking on Him
Price of Passion
Investing in Love
Knowing Your Worth

Treasured Forever
Banking on Christmas
Billionaire Banker Box Set Books #1-3

Billionaire CEO Brothers
Tempting the Player
Late Night Boardroom
Reviewing the Perfomance
Result of Passion
Directing the Next Move
Touching the Assets

Billionaire Hitman Series
The Hit
The Job
The Run

Billionaire Holiday Romance Series
Driving Home for Christmas
The Valentine Getaway
Cruising Love
Billionaire Holiday Romance Box Set

Billionaire in Disguise Series
Facade
Illusion

Charade

Billionaire Secrets Series
The Secret
Freedom
Courage
Trust
Impulse
Billionaire Secrets Box Set Books #1-3

Blind Sight Series
See Me
Fix Me
Eyes On Me

Branded Series
Money or Nothing
What People Say
Give and Take

Building Billions
Building Billions - Part 1
Building Billions - Part 2
Building Billions - Part 3

Butler & Heiress Series
To Serve
For Duty
No Chore
All Wrapped Up

Change of Heart Series
The Heart Needs
The Heart Wants
The Heart Knows

Club Confession Series
Envy
Crave
Decoy
Urge
Oath
Club Confession Box Set Books #1-3

Cottage by the Sea Series
Surging Tide
Distant Shores
Twisting Ocean

Counting the Billions
Counting the Days
Counting On You
Counting the Kisses

Cry Wolf Reverse Harem Series
Beautiful & Wild
Misunderstood
Never Tamed

Darkest Night Series
Savage
Vicious
Brutal
Sinful
Fierce

Department of Defense Series
Dead Ahead

Diamond in the Rough Anthology
Billionaire Rock
Billionaire Rock - part 2

Dirty Little Taboo Series
Flirting Touch
Denying Pleasure
Forbidding Desire
Craving Passion

Dominating PA Series
Her Personal Assistant - Part 1
Her Personal Assistant - Part 2
Her Personal Assistant Box Set

Fake Billionaire Series
Faking It
Temporary CEO
Caught in the Act
Never Tell A Lie
Fake Christmas
Fake Billionaire Box Set #1-3

Firehouse Romance Series
Caught in Flames
Burning With Desire
Craving the Heat
Firehouse Romance Complete Collection

Forging Billions Series
Dirty Money
Petty Cash
Payment Required

For His Pleasure
Elizabeth
Georgia
Madison

Fortune Riders MC Series
Billionaire Biker
Billionaire Ransom
Billionaire Misery
Fortune Riders Box Set - Books #1-3

Fragile Series
Fragile Touch
Fragile Kiss
Fragile Love

Great Temptation Series
The Devil's Footsteps
Heaven's Command

Mortals Surrender

Hades' Spawn Motorcycle Club
One You Can't Forget
One That Got Away
One That Came Back
One You Never Leave
One Christmas Night
Hades' Spawn MC Complete Series

Hard Rocked Series
Rhyme
Harmony
Lyrics

Heart of Stone Series
The Protector
The Guardian
The Warrior

Heart of the Battle Series
Celtic Viking
Celtic Rune
Celtic Mann
Heart of the Battle Series Box Set

Heistdom Series
Master Thief
Goldmine
Diamond Heist
Smile For Me
Your Move
Green With Envy
Saving Money

Highlander Wolf Series
Pack Run
Pack Land
Pack Rules

Hollyweird Fae Series
Inception of Gold
Disruption of Magic
Guardians of Twilight

How To Love A Spy
The Secret
The Secret Life
The Secret Wife

Just About Series
About Love
About Truth
About Forever
Just About Box Set Books #1-3

Justice Series
Seeking Justice
Finding Justice
Chasing Justice
Pursuing Justice
Justice - Complete Series

Karma Series
Walk Away
Make Him Pay
Perfect Revenge

King of Hades MC Series
Sinner
Tempting Sinner
Enticing Sinner

Kissed by Billions

Kissed by Passion
Kissed by Desire
Kissed by Love

Leaning Towards Trouble
Trouble
Discord
Tenacity

Love on the Sea Series
Ships Ahoy
Rough Sea
High Tide

Lovers in London Series
Risking Millions
Venture Capital
Worth the Expense
The Price of Luxury
Exclusive Passion
Sparkling Christmas
Lovers in London - 3 Book Box Set

Love You Series
Love Life
Need Love

My Love

Managing the Billionaire
Never Enough
Worth the Cost
Secret Admirers
Chasing Affection
Pressing Romance
Timeless Memories
Managing the Billionaire Box Set Books #1-3

Managing the Bosses Series
The Boss
The Boss Too
Who's the Boss Now
Love the Boss
I Do the Boss
Wife to the Boss
Employed by the Boss
Brother to the Boss
Senior Advisor to the Boss
Forever the Boss
Christmas With the Boss
Billionaire in Control
Billionaire Makes Millions
Billionaire at Work
Precious Little Thing
Priceless Love
Valentine Love
The Cost of Freedom

Trick or Treat
The Night Before Christmas
Gift for the Boss - Novella 3.5
Managing the Bosses Box Set #1-3
Managing the Bosses Novellas

Mislead by the Bad Boy Series
Deceived
Provoked
Betrayed

Model Mayhem Series
Shameless
Modesty
Imperfection

Moment in Time
Highlander's Bride
Victorian Bride
Modern Day Bride
A Royal Bride
Forever the Bride

Mountain Millionaire Series
Close to the Ridge
Crossing the Bluff

Climbing the Mount

My Best Friend's Sister
Hometown Calling
A Perfect Moment
Thrown in Together

My Darker Side Series
Darkest Hour
Time to Stop
Against the Light

Neverending Dream Series
Neverending Dream - Part 1
Neverending Dream - Part 2
Neverending Dream - Part 3
Neverending Dream - Part 4
Neverending Dream - Part 5
Neverending Dream Box Set Books #1-3

Outside the Octagon
Submit
Fight
Knockout

Protecting Diana Series
Her Bodyguard
Her Defender
Her Champion
Her Protector
Her Forever
Protecting Diana Box Set Books #1-3

Protecting Layla Series
His Mission
His Objective
His Devotion

Racing Hearts Series
Rush
Pace
Fast

Regency Romance Series
The Duchess Scandal - Part 1
The Duchess Scandal - Part 2

Reverse Harem Series
Primals

Archaic
Unitary

Roommate Wanted Series
The Roommate
The Bunkmate
The Flatmate

R&S Rich and Single Series
Alex Reid
Parker
Sebastian
Zane

Saving Forever
Saving Forever - Part 1
Saving Forever - Part 2
Saving Forever - Part 3
Saving Forever - Part 4
Saving Forever - Part 5
Saving Forever - Part 6
Saving Forever Part 7
Saving Forever - Part 8
Saving Forever Boxset Books #1-3

Secrets & Lies Series

Strange Secrets
Evading Secrets
Inspiring Secrets
Lies and Secrets
Mastering Secrets
Alluring Secrets
Secrets & Lies Box Set Books #1-3

Shifting Desires Series
Jungle Heat
Jungle Fever
Jungle Blaze

Sin Series
Payment for Sin
Atonement Within
Declaration of Love

Southern Romance Series
Little Love Affair
Siege of the Heart
Freedom Forever
Soldier's Fortune

Spanked Series
Passion

Playmate
Pleasure

Spelling Love Series
The Author
The Book Boyfriend
The Words of Love

Strength & Style
Suits You, Sir
Tailor Made
Perfect Gentleman

Taboo Wedding Series
He Loves Me Not
With This Ring
Happily Ever After

Tattooist Series
Confession of a Tattooist
Surrender of a Tattooist
Heart of a Tattooist
Hopes & Dreams of a Tattooist

Tennessee Romance

Whisky Lullaby
Whisky Melody
Whisky Harmony

The Bad Boy Alpha Club
Battle Lines - Part 1
Battle Lines

The Brush Of Love Series
Every Night
Every Day
Every Time
Every Way
Every Touch
The Brush of Love Series Box Set Books #1-3

The City of Mayhem Series
True Mayhem
Relentless Chaos
Broken Disorder

The Coffee Shop Romance Series
A Rich Aftertaste

The Debt

The Debt: Part 1 - Damn Horse
The Debt: Complete Collection

The Fire Inside Series
Dare Me
Defy Me
Burn Me

The Gentleman's Club Series
Gambler
Player
Wager

The Golden Game
On The Pitch
Respect the Game
All Game
Sweat and Tears
The Final Score
The Golden Game Box Set Books #1-3

The Golden Mail
Hot Off the Press
Extra! Extra!
Read All About It
Stop the Press

Breaking News
This Just In
The Golden Mail Box Set Books #1-3

The Long Con Series
The Misfit
The Hustle
The Cheat

The Lucky Billionaire Series
Lucky Break
Streak of Luck
Lucky in Love

The Millionaire's Pretty Woman Series
Perfect Stranger
Captive Devotion
Sweet Temptations

The Sound of Breaking Hearts Series
Disruption
Destroy
Devoted

The University of Gatica Series

The Recruiting Trip
Faster
Higher
Stronger
Dominate
No Rush
University of Gatica - The Complete Series

The Wrong Side of the Tracks
The Knockback
The Overshare
The Fightback

Timing is Everything Series
Right Time
Right Place
Right Reasons

T.N.T. Series
Troubled Nate Thomas - Part 1
Troubled Nate Thomas - Part 2
Troubled Nate Thomas - Part 3

Toxic Touch Series
Noxious
Lethal

Willful
Tainted
Craved
Toxic Touch Box Set Books #1-3

Undercover Boss Series
Marketing
Finance
Legal

Undercover Series
Perfect For Me
Perfect For You
Perfect For Us

Unknown Identity Series
Unknown
Unpublished
Unexposed
Unsure
Unwritten
Unknown Identity Box Set: Books #1-3

Unlucky Series
Unlucky in Love
UnWanted

UnLoved Forever

War Torn Letters Series
My Sweetheart
My Darling
My Beloved

Wet & Wild Series
Stormy Love
Savage Love
Secure Love

Worth It Series
Worth Billions
Worth Every Cent
Worth More Than Money

You & Me - A Bad Boy Romance
Just Me
Touch Me
Kiss Me

Standalone
Wash
Loving Charity

Summer Lovin'
Love & College
Billionaire Heart
First Love
Frisky and Fun Romance Box Collection
Beating Hades' Bikers
Everyone Loves a Bad Boy
Dead of Night

About the Author

"Love should be something that lasts forever, not is lost forever." Visit USA TODAY BESTSELLING AUTHOR, LEXY TIMMS https://www.facebook.com/SavingForever *Please feel free to connect with me and share your comments. I love connecting with my readers.* Sign up for news and updates and freebies - I like spoiling my readers! http://eepurl.com/9i0vD website: www.lexytimms.com Dealing in Antique Jewelry and hanging out with her awesome hubby and three kids, Lexy Timms loves writing in her free time. MANAGING THE BOSSES is a bestselling 10-part series dipping into the lives of Alex Reid and Jamie Connors. Can a secretary really fall for her billionaire boss?

Read more at www.lexytimms.com.